MUSIC

OF THE

SOUL

a novel

Gail Miller Mahaffey

ISBN 978-1-63630-318-5 (Paperback)
ISBN 978-1-63630-319-2 (Hardcover)
ISBN 978-1-63630-320-8 (Digital)

Covenant Books, Inc.
11661 Hwy 707
Murrells Inlet, SC 29576
www.covenantbooks.com

for Mary Beth

PROLOGUE

You are the music while the music lasts.

—T.S.Eliot

Spring 1988

Torrents of rain were hitting the windshield of Donald Mason's car amidst the thickening fog, making it impossible to see past the hood ornament that sat on the nose of his vehicle. The wind howled like a wolf in search of its prey.

"Drive slower, Donald. You're going too fast," Ann Mason yelled as she nibbled nervously on what was left of her already gnawed fingernails. "The roads are slippery, Donald," she shouted with a frightening tone in her voice. "Please slow down! You're making me nervous."

The nagging remarks shouted from Donald Mason's wife made him want to speed up in response to her often negative comments, but the pounding rain hitting the windshield with incredible force was a nonstop reminder that that would not be the proper action to take in response to the bite of her tongue. The windshield wipers swiftly going back and forth barely helped him see ahead as the storm raged on with a furry that shook his usually calm demeanor.

"I'm doing the best I can, Ann. Please let me drive."

A growing tension hung in the air. Donald gripped the wheel tighter with frozen hands, as if this would give him more control of the car and more control of his wife's contrary comments. The rain would not let up. The wind blew with a sneering defiance.

They were on the interstate. A fierce nor'easter was ripping through the area.

"Donald, please!"

"Anne, stop your incessant bickering and—"

Red lights suddenly lit up between the blur of raindrops in front of them followed by the sound of screeching brakes, crumbling metal, and splintering glass. Donald applied the brakes swiftly, making the car spin around several times before it crashed into the one in front of them with brutal force. What was left of their vehicle and the others in front of it rolled down the side of the mud-slick hillside and into the ravine below. The sickening sight of maimed vehicles and exploding gas tanks filled the field below. There were bodies, motionless bodies. Among them lay Donald. Next to him lay the body of his wife, her face frozen in horror. And then after the exploding stopped and the burning subsided, there was silence, pure silence. The wolf had taken its prey. It gloated with pride.

1

After silence, that which comes nearest to
expressing the inexpressible is music.

—Aldous Huxley

D ressed in a floor-length silky black sheath, with her hair piled high on top of her head, Meredith Mason looked gorgeous. But gorgeous didn't do anything to relieve the stress and anguish that was building up inside of her as she nervously paced to and fro backstage at the Eastman Performance Theatre. Performing did not make her nervous. It was second nature to her. The act of performing was in her blood, and the expectation of it always created a wonderful sense of yearning and excitement that could only be satisfied by getting onstage and sharing her music with her audience. Then and only then would she experience the golden glory of being entirely in her element. It was pure joy, and she loved it.

She was nervous because her parents had not yet arrived and were driving in the midst of a raging storm. The howl of the wind and the heavy beating of the raindrops on the windows of the building were shear testament to the severity of the nor'easter that forecasters had been predicting would be one of the worst in years to hit the area. Maybe they had pulled off the road somewhere. Maybe they were just unable to get here on time. They had seen her perform numerous times, and maybe they were just playing it safe. The wind blew extra hard, making the windows rattle, and blew away with it her hopes that they were okay.

She skipped her normal preconcert preparations in hopes that she could see her parents before the concert began. But that wasn't going to happen. After taking the remaining few minutes left to compose herself, she walked onstage beneath the bright lights with confidence, as her audience smiled and clapped with admiration. She sat down on the bench in front of the shiny large piano before her and mentally focused every bit of energy and concentration that was inside of her on what she was about to do. Her brain was clear. The fire was inside her. And then she began. She was the music. She became the music. She was gloriously in her element and it showed. The audience was in for a grand ride, and they knew it from the moment she began. She was sheer magic. What was to follow the magic for Meredith would be pure hell.

The excitement and fun of performing was over. A long wait followed by the eventual phone call. Reality set in. The disbelief. The denial. The fantasy of trying not to accept what was really real. The unimaginable had happened, and the feelings of disbelief set in. How could this happen to her? Her success had been so perfect. Her life had been perfect. Things like this didn't happen to people like her. Or did they?

The anguish was unbearable. As the days and weeks went by, there was this huge hole inside of her that seemingly could not be filled by anything. It gnawed at her insides, leaving a sick feeling that wouldn't go away. It never subsided even for a minute's relief. How could she live with this burrowing deep within her?

She was at the ending point of a part of her life that should have been full of joy. She should have been pursuing the next chapter with excitement and enthusiasm instead of carrying with her the baggage of grief, guilt, and sadness. Yes, baggage. It was truly baggage. If her parent's death had happened in any other way, she would not have felt responsible. She would not have felt the heavy burden of guilt that she carried on her shoulders. They died coming to see her. If they hadn't tried to come, they would still be alive. Everything would have been all right. They would be alive, and her life would have gone on as expected: Graduate school. Performances. Perfection.

Now, her music was her only relief. She dove into it and held onto its safety like a drowning person hanging on to a life preserver. It became her life preserver. It became the only place where she could find comfort and beauty and peace. While emerged in her music, there was no death. There was no guilt. There was only the joy it brought her. It became her refuge and her strength. It would not fail her the way life had failed her. It would lead the way, and she would hold on to it and follow it where ever it led her.

Could she go on following its lead? Where would it take her?

2

A painter paints pictures on canvas. But
musicians paint their pictures on silence.
—Leopold Stokowski

Fall 1995

And so it was with Meredith. Seemingly effortless and with feeling, she poured her sense of beauty and pain into the floating melodies of sound that drifted upward from her instrument. A giver and
a sharer, she unleashed her experience of the essence of being upon
the canvas of life with her music. Confidence resulting from mastery
of her craft emanated from the stage of her concert halls like the rush
of a mountain stream from the height of a mountain. She would take
her place at the piano before a performance, head held high and eyes
sparkling with eager brilliance. She would charismatically capture the
ears and hearts of all present. Audiences sat in mummified silence as
they listened to the mesmerizing notes that she magically wove into
a musical tapestry of brilliant colors right before their eyes. This was
how she delivered her music and her love to the world, and the world
was listening.

Meredith Mason sat pensively staring out the floor-to-ceiling
picture window of her second-floor piano studio in the two-story
brick building at the Converse College School of Music. Her long,
slender fingers rested on the shiny row of ivory keys stretched out in
front of her on the giant, well-polished Steinway that was hers to use
as professor of music at the prestigious school where she taught. She
was thinking of her life thus far and all that she had achieved and
where she was headed in the near future. She had accomplished what

most aspiring young musicians only dreamed of. Envied by her peers and equaled by few, she was performing as a soloist on a national level, in demand as a concert pianist. Despite practically an entire lifetime devoted to perfecting her technique at the piano through endless hours of practice, playing and performing had always come easily to her from the beginning. Her playing was something she loved to do, and it brought her immense pleasure. She was gifted with an almost spiritual connection to her music that could be immediately shared with a listening audience. Her music came from a deep, sensitive place within her soul. She could get intensely lost in her playing, musically sharing emotions and feelings that she couldn't even begin to communicate verbally through conversation. She was a true artist in every way. Mastery of her flawless technique made it possible to pour creative expression and vivid excitement into the lifeless black notes that appeared in front of her upon the printed page. She excited her audiences and brought them with her on her musical journeys.

At the young age of only twenty-nine, Meredith was already a full professor of music in piano performance, with an impressive resume and education. But no one knew. No one knew the pain she carried deep inside of her. It was there all the time, but no one could see it. Even the people she worked with didn't know. The guilt of the death of her parents had buried itself deep within her soul. It would not leave. It gnawed away at her insides. In reality, it was the reason for her incredible success. But no one knew. People could only hear the beauty of her music, which was her connection with life. Life flowed through her music, and her music was all the people cared about. That was all she allowed anyone to see. It was her joy and her anchor. It was life itself to her.

Performing was not something Meredith simply wanted to do. She was compelled to do it. Lodged deep within her soul was a yearning to play that had to be satisfied by performing. Playing alone and losing herself in her music was deeply satisfying in itself, but sharing what she created in front of an audience fed the hunger that lay deep within her. It was a passion. It was a craving. It was something she had to do. She had this God-given talent and couldn't exist without exploring and sharing it with the numerous but faceless bodies who filled the rows and rows of seats in the concert halls where she played. Sharing her music completed her in a way that nothing else could. It filled her soul and united her with her spirit. And it helped her deal with and cover up her grief.

Being at Julliard for her graduate work had been magnificent, and she had loved the hustle and bustle of New York City life, where she could take in a museum or a show or feast at a fabulous restaurant at a moment's notice. But now she was ready to leave the city and yearned for a smaller, quieter place—a place where she could settle down, a place she could call home. She hoped to find a college town where she could teach but still have the opportunity to jet off to exciting places and feed her desire to perform.

The job at Converse College came up quickly and suddenly at the end of her time at Julliard. She was recruited by the dean of the School of Music, who was totally impressed when he accidently heard her perform with the Charlotte Symphony. After hearing her play, he was determined to have her come to the school for an interview and sign her on to fill the open slot in his piano faculty. He had no idea if she was pursuing a job, but he sought her out and desperately wanted to convince her to come to Converse. Someone of her caliber would be a bonus for his school, attracting many students who otherwise might choose to attend colleges and universities elsewhere to study with well-known teachers. She had made quite a name for herself so far in her career, and young piano students looking at colleges for their education would grab at the opportunity to study with her. She was a fresh, new face in the performing world, who could light up a stage with her talent and motivate these new young students yearning to be like her.

Meredith accepted the interview at Converse College in Spartanburg, a small but culturally exciting town in the upstate of South Carolina. She was captivated by the charm and amenities of the little village that was nestled between the North Carolina mountains and the South Carolina low country. The town itself boasted a ballet company, a professional symphony orchestra, and an impressive cultural center, which often hosted national touring companies of many Broadway shows and musicals. It had the amenities of a big city, including an international airport, and the charm of a delightfully interesting small town.

Built in 1889, Converse College was surrounded by the quaint historic neighborhood of Converse Heights built mainly in the early 1900s. The post-Victorian village contained a splendid variety of uniquely restored homes, which were surrounded by neatly manicured gardens and lovely giant old trees. It was a little jewel of a town unknown to most people who lived elsewhere in the state.

Meredith accepted the job quickly, immediately falling in love with the college and its quaint post-Victorian surroundings. She was able to purchase a small, darling little newly restored home in Converse Heights. Her inheritance from her parents had allowed her the flexibility to buy rather than rent, and she had been delighted with her purchase.

Meredith sat looking out her studio window, which looked upon a well-treed courtyard of the campus. The ancient oak trees that had been majestic pillars of sticks just a few weeks earlier were now sprouting tiny buds that would soon bloom into the lettuce-green foliage of early spring. Students walking to class below were wearing light jackets instead of the wooly coats and scarves that had kept them warm a little more than a month before. She stared with delight at the charming college campus peopled with an interesting and diverse student population and a faculty Meredith was proud to be a part of.

A knock at the door startled Meredith and brought her back to the present. "Oh hello, Dr. Preston," she said cheerfully.

"Hello, Meredith. I just wanted to tell someone I'm leaving for the day, in case a wandering student comes looking for me. They always seem to appear at my door like lost sheep whenever I leave early," he confided.

"I'll be glad to tend the flock for you," beamed Meredith. I'll be here a while longer working on the Rachmaninoff. I feel like I'm really getting into the spirit of the piece now."

"That's great," beamed Dr. Preston. "I'll be excited to hear your interpretation. I know it will be impressive. But go easy on yourself! Make sure you get some dinner! I'll see you in the morning."

"I will," promised Meredith." I'll just work a bit longer," she added. Waving goodbye, he left the room, moving down the hall with his usual quick paced stride that was both businesslike and professional.

Bill Preston's office was just down the hall from Meredith's studio. He was the dean of the School of Music and director of the Spartanburg Philharmonic, the small but impressive local orchestra composed mainly of paid professionals, in addition to a few advanced collegiate players. Through the years, he had molded the orchestra into the prestigious, well-respected group that it was today. He personally had recruited Meredith for the piano faculty and felt like he had won the prize when she accepted the position. The other candidates who interviewed for the job did not have the resume of glowing brilliance that made Meredith stand out like a golden needle in a haystack. Needless to say, he was overjoyed when she was eager and enthusiastic to sign her contract. It included playing the Rachmaninoff *Piano Concerto No. 2* at the opening concert with the Philharmonic in the fall. Bill Preston was thrilled, but it was Meredith who felt she had won the prize. Being able to live, work, and teach in the delightful little area known as Converse Heights while still being able to perform in far-off places was exactly what she had wanted for her future.

Meredith put her fingers to the keys and began working on a difficult passageway that was midway into the first movement of the piece. She slowed the passage down and went over and over the intricate fingering that would eventually be played without thought to the mechanics of it all. After mastering the section, she took the piece up to tempo, adding her own interpretation of what the composer was trying to say while becoming totally lost in the captive spell of what she was playing. The music became food for her craving, totally satiating her, allowing her to live totally in the present and forget the past. Meredith sat and played for what could have been hours, unaware of the amount of time that had passed. Her only awareness was that of the pleasure that encompassed her as she played.

Two luminous large brown eyes shined with obvious excitement while rich long brown hair rhythmically swayed from side to side with every musical innuendo. Meredith Mason was a rare beauty in disguise. Her reserved personality often prevented people from noticing her, and the regal qualities of her perfectly formed facial features were often hidden by her dangling thick hair. Today, it hung loose and wild and unencumbered, dancing however it willed. Meredith's spirit was like her frolicking hair. It was beautiful and free and uninhibited. It danced within the music, expressing itself in unleashed joy, charging ahead full force like a cavalry of horses set loose in a field. She became the joy. She became the excitement. She became the music. She was in her element, and she glowed from within. Any presence of sadness or regret was gone when she played. If it would only stay away for good. How could she make it stay away for good? How could she rid herself of the guilt and pain that she carried inside herself?

3

A man should hear a little music…every day of his life,
in order that worldly cares may not obliterate the sense
of the beautiful which God has implanted in the
human soul.
                              —John Wolfgang von Goethe

Shadows were lengthening from the tall trees lining the courtyard outside Meredith's studio. The shimmery streaks of sunlight glimmered through the branches of the giant oaks as the sun descended in the west toward its evening resting place. The golden pool of yellow melted slowly into the thin bowl of the horizon. Dusk was coming to the Carolinas with its confirmation that life, with all of its fury and busyness, should be gilded with the glow of peace and stillness that evening brought.

Meredith's stomach began growling from hunger and transported her from her musical trance into the present. She realized she needed food and gathered her belongings to take with her as she decided to leave for the evening. Grabbing the large brown leather shoulder strap of her purse, she put on her wooly thigh-length sweater, turned out the lights, and locked the door to her second-story studio. She flew down the stairs and ran out the back door to the faculty parking lot, where her little red VW convertible sat waiting for her beneath the trees in the fading light of the setting sun.

After turning on the ignition, she pulled out onto South Fairview Street and made a right onto East Main, where she turned into the parking lot of Ice Cream and Coffee Beans, a little café that served up delicate treats for the discriminating palate, including gourmet soups, salads, and sandwiches. It was late, and she didn't have the energy to prepare anything to eat at home, so takeout was the perfect choice. She ordered her Southern favorite, a pimento cheese sandwich with jalapeño peppers on grilled sourdough bread, and completed the order with a cup of homemade vegetable soup, some kettle chips, and a sweet tea. She had only lived in the South for a few months but had already developed a taste for several Southern delicacies. Sweet tea was one Southern favorite she relished. New Yorkers had no idea what sweet tea was or how addictive it could become. Up North, if you ordered tea, you got hot tea in a cup and saucer. If you ordered iced tea, you got unsweetened cold tea with ice cubes. Only in the South did some people choose one restaurant over another because it had good tea. Somewhere across America, going east to west was the sweet tea line. If you crossed it going North, you were looked at as if you were a bit crazy if you asked for sweet tea. If you crossed it going South, you got sweet tea whether you asked for it or not. It was as sure a demarcation as was the equator or the continental divide. No one seemed to know exactly where it was, but many a Southerner had been irritated into an irrational rage when not able to order sweet tea in a restaurant on the wrong side of the line. Northerners could not understand that putting sugar into a glass of cold tea would never be the same as tea that had been presweetened with sugar while it was still hot.

Meredith carefully grabbed the bag containing her Southern dinner, jumped into her little red convertible, drove out of the parking lot, and made the right turn onto Mills Avenue in Converse Heights. Another turn onto Palmetto Street brought her to the cute little bungalow-style house she had been able to purchase, completely renovated and in move-in condition. The outside was painted a soft sage green with white trim complimented by black shutters and doors. A black wooden rocker sat on each side of the front porch. Giant clay pots on either side of the doorway would soon be filled with lush red geraniums when the warm weather set in. A stone chimney climbed up the side wall toward the sky, which was partially hidden by the many large oak trees surrounding the bungalow. It was a picture-perfect home, and she loved it.

Inside in the living room was the baby grand piano that was hers since her childhood. Her parents had lovingly purchased it for her when they discovered Meredith was serious about pursuing a musical career and that she had the talent to go with her enthusiasm. They would have been thoroughly proud of Meredith and the successful career she had built for herself through hard work and sheer talent.

She plopped her yummy meal down on the kitchen table, took off her wooly sweater, and began to devour the Southern feast. Life was good, she thought, as she savored a bit of the pimento cheese on her palate. So much was right, yet in addition to the trauma she buried deep within her from the death of her parents, she harbored a sense of loneliness inside of her that at times forced its way to the top of her feelings. It created a certain sadness that could be depressing if she didn't force herself to be such an optimist. Her almost obsessive push to rise to the top of her career had left her without friends, mainly because she never seemed to have the time to cultivate any. Now, being almost thirty and an incredible success in the music world, she felt almost shy and awkward in one-on-one social situations with other people. The bold confidence that was so present on stage was glaringly lacking in her personal life. Here she was, at seven thirty in the evening, with good food, a beautiful house, and no one to talk to. There was no girl friend to call and share confidences with, no mother to offer comfort, not even a pet to hug and scratch on the head, although that could be the most fixable of all the problems. And there was no man. There never had been a man. She had always been too busy to acknowledge the attention of any man, as few and far between as any offers of attention had been. She never felt she needed a man, or for that matter even a friend, to achieve her goal of musical success. Now having achieved the golden prize of rising to the top, in addition to bearing her grief, she was lonely.

There was really no one on the music faculty whom she really felt she could bond with in a personal way. Dr. Preston had been her only friend. But he was more of a mentor in a fatherly way than a friend. He was married and in his fifties, graying at the temples and handsome in a way that was becoming to someone his age. Having raised two boys of his own, he had been dean of the music faculty and conductor of the Philharmonic for twenty-three years. Meredith found him to be kind, wise, and musically gifted; and she had great admiration for his talent. She realized he was determined to help her further her career in any way that he could, and she was pleased to work for a man of his caliber. Other handsome, available men just didn't seem to work at the college. At least she didn't think so. So once again, her career was the dominant focus in her life. And it filled her with what she needed in the present. But something was always missing deep inside.

Meredith disposed of the paper and plastic from her takeout dinner, brushing crumbs from the counter and tidying up as she cleaned. The house was all too perfect. She needed someone to share it with, someone to talk to, just someone. Oh well. Having practiced much of the day, she felt she deserved some hang loose time this evening. After a warm, soothing bubble bath, she dressed in her lace-trimmed flannel granny gown and curled up in bed with a good book and a glass of red wine, pulling her goose down comforter up to her chin to keep herself toasty warm and comfortable. A *Chopin Etudes* CD softly played in the background, setting the stage for a restful night's sleep after a busy day.

4

Music produces a kind of pleasure which
human nature cannot do without.
—Confucius

Spring came to the area in all its majesty. The blooming began in ritualistic order, as it did every year, allowing each species or plant to bask in solo before the blooming of the next variety. First came the daffodils sprouting up in every yard. They almost made a path through the area like the one Dorothy followed down the yellow brick road. The Bradford pears came next, along with the white-and-pink cherry blossoms, turning the area into a snowy-like wonderland. Then as if touched by a fairy's magic wand, the pinks and whites and reds of the azaleas appeared, crowned by the blooming of the dogwoods, sprinkling their color on the sides of the streets. Traffic picked up in the area as visitors slowly drove through the streets, examining the glorious display of color, the way they examined the area at Christmas time for decorations. Meredith felt like a fairy princess as she drove through her kingdom on her way to the college each day.

Summer brought the blooming of the white, pink, and red crepe myrtle trees. Warm morning temperatures were followed by steamy afternoons, but this particular summer, not being a very humid one, Meredith was able to sit on her back screened porch in the evenings with the ceiling fan on. The shade from the giant trees provided extra coolness in the yard and made the porch a nice evening retreat. As the sun set, the huge number of fireflies made the yard look as if it were filled with dozens of blinking trees at Christmastime. The fireflies brought back fond memories of trying to catch the bugs in a mason jar as a child, only to let them free a few minutes later. The music of the crickets, locusts, and summer bugs drifted from yard to yard, creating an intricate symphony that would crescendo and decrescendo in peaks and valleys of sound. To the listening ear, each insect could be individually heard as it took its turn to sing with delight above the others, seeming to carry the main theme of the piece the way an instrument in the orchestra would do. The harmony of the different textures of sound brought joy to the audience of porch dwellers, enjoying the warm summer evenings.

Meredith's teaching schedule was light in the summertime. Only a few of her regular students remained in town for lessons in the summer, so she had lots of free time to work on the Rachmaninoff and other pieces of her choosing. Four to six hours of daily practice time was the minimum for a concert pianist. It was a time to freely dive into her music, refine her technique, and enjoy putting her personal expression into the pieces she felt she had mastered. It was a time to be alone with her music, and she loved it.

One particular Monday, she had no students coming in for lessons, so she dressed in jeans, sandals, and a worn "I Love New York" T-shirt. Her hair was twisted and secured in the back with a yellow no. 2 pencil, and various other strands of her hair hung down on her forehead, hiding her giant brown eyes and naturally pink complexion. She wore no makeup that morning and was delighted to feel relaxed as she got to her studio and began working on the Rachmaninoff. The basic technical work was complete, and she was now able to work on putting in the emotional expression, which was the part she loved the most.

A knock at the door came at the fury of an ascending passageway. The creaking of the door opening startled Meredith and brought her back to reality. She turned and saw Dr. Preston entering with a handsome tall man who appeared to be in his early thirties. He was dressed in neat khaki pants and a light-blue tailored shirt covered by a dark navy blazer. His sandy brown hair was neatly cut, and a dimple on each side of his mouth appeared as he gave a little smile at Meredith in her college student attire.

"Dr. Mason. Meredith," stammered Dr. Preston, staring at the yellow wooden pencil stuck in her hair like a chopstick. "I'd like you to meet Evan Sanders. We are borrowing him from the Asheville Symphony at the beginning of the fall semester, and he will help fill out our cello section for the Rachmaninoff. He currently teaches at UNC Asheville and will be a fine addition to our group." Evan smiled again and held out a friendly hand to Meredith, as she looked at him, surprised but pleased to meet him. His handshake was strong and firm, and his smile was warm and friendly.

"Dr. Mason," he began.

"No, please, it's Meredith," she insisted. "It's so nice to meet you and have you play with the Philharmonic for the concert."

"Meredith came to us from Julliard this past winter," beamed Dr. Preston proudly like a doting father. "She will perform the Rachmaninoff in our fall lineup of concerts. She is a magnificent addition to our piano faculty."

"I'm sure she is," replied Evan. "The passages I heard when we entered were quite inspiring!"

"Thank you," replied Meredith bashfully. "I'm sorry I didn't hear you knock. I'm afraid I tend to get quite caught up in my playing at times!"

"That's a good thing," Evan remarked.

Doctor Preston placed his hand on the doorknob. "We're taking our tour of the building. Just wanted to drop in so you two would be familiar with each other." Waiving briefly, he stepped out into the hall. Evan flashed his radiant smile at Meredith once more, and she quickly waived as they left the room. After they were gone, Meredith stood up and stared at herself in the long mirror that hung on the other side of her piano. Good grief! She would have to be dressed like a student on the day she was introduced to the only attractive male presence in the building! She brushed the long straggles of hair out of her eyes and gazed upon the tacky "I Love New York" T-shirt she wore, which was stained from the latte she had picked up at Ice Cream and Coffee Beans that morning. She made a mental note to do better with her dress on her days off from now on.

The days that followed found Meredith trying to dress more professionally to look like the respected faculty member that she was, but she had not seen Evan Sanders in the building at all since their first introduction. The students were filtering back to the campus in dribbles, but classes for the fall term did not begin until the following Monday. Freshman orientation was currently going on. The students who were being herded through the building led by upper-class tour guides looked young, immature, and slightly apprehensive about the new life they were beginning. Meredith adored teaching her older students. They were deeply dedicated to their musical careers and always came well prepared to their lessons. It was fun to work with them individually, drawing out the musicality she knew was buried deep inside each one. She tried to encourage and inspire. She wanted to develop their musical ear so they knew what it was they were reaching for. She would get physically excited during her lessons, jumping up and down with joy as her students reached new levels of achievement. She would demonstrate passageways for them or play with them to draw their musicality to the surface. She would do whatever it took, and the students loved her for all of her energy and enthusiasm.

It was the new freshmen she was concerned about. She hoped she would not receive any students who lacked the discipline to put in the endless hours of practice it takes to become a musician. Most of the students who were admitted here were born with a considerable amount of raw talent, but it was talent that had to be molded and developed through practice. The students were the clay, and she was the potter. Her job was to help them find themselves and express themselves musically, developing their technique while not destroying their innate creativity. She extracted what was there and helped them turn it into a masterpiece.

Monday arrived, and with it came the first day of classes. Meredith came dressed in a soft gray tunic-length linen pant suit complimented by a paisley silk scarf and chunky-heeled espadrilles. Her long silky brown hair was neatly brushed behind her ears. She wore the tiny pair of silver pierced earrings that she always wore to complete her outfits. Her students were coming by her studio informally to sign up for lesson times, some just meeting her for the first time. She seemed impressed with the caliber of the new students and enjoyed conversing with her returning students she had not taught during summer session. As she was standing at the piano, surveying her nearly completed schedule, there was a knock at the open door.

"Hello there!" It was Evan Sanders, smiling once again at Meredith as he entered confidently.

"Oh, hi!" beamed Meredith, happy to see that he had remembered her and where her studio was. She stepped out from behind the piano.

"You must be here for the first meeting of the collegiate symphony later today."

"That's right," replied Evan, "but I'll mainly be observing today to check out the cello section. Dr. Preston wants me to do some sectionals with the students eventually, but not at the moment." Evan gave her an amusing look.

"What's the matter? Don't you love New York today?" Meredith blushed a thousand shades of red when she realized that he had remembered the tacky outfit she had been wearing on the day they met.

"Well, I always love New York, I just don't usually go broadcasting the fact to everyone in such a bold manner." They both laughed, and Meredith blushed again.

Evan seemed to have a relaxed, warm manner that made him easy to talk to. She was pleased that he had stopped in to chat and pleasantly noticed she didn't feel awkward with him at all.

"Will you be here every day?" she asked.

"No," he replied, "just twice a week for a while. I'll still be working at the University in Asheville the other days until we get closer to the performance. How about you?" Evan asked. "Will you be rehearsing with the symphony yet?"

"No, not yet," she said. "They'll throw me in the last week of rehearsals when the student orchestra is ready and the professionals join in. That will be the fun part for me."

"I'm really looking forward to it." Evan looked at her, hoping for a positive response.

"I'll be back on Wednesday. How about doing lunch? Can you squeeze it into your busy schedule?" Meredith smiled pleasantly, as a little thrill of excitement ran up and down her spine.

"I'd like that very much. Actually, my regular schedule of lessons doesn't begin until next week, so this week is quite free." Evan poked fun at her again and asked if she happened to have a no. 2 pencil he could borrow to write down her phone number. She made a face at him, and he laughed back at her. She told him this was war and that she would eventually get him back good. They exchanged numbers and quickly said their goodbyes. Evan had a four o'clock symphony meeting, and Meredith had a faculty meeting. As he left, Meredith smiled inside, pleased with her newly acquired friend and looking forward to lunch on Wednesday.

5

Music is the poetry of the air.

—Jean Paul Richter

Wednesday came, and Meredith tried several outfits on before deciding what to wear for her lunch with Evan. A long, straight linen chambray skirt with a hip-length matching sleeveless vest and elbow-length white button-down cotton shirt would be perfect. Beige sandals completed her outfit as did her signature silver earrings she almost always wore. Evan appeared at her studio at eleven forty-five sharp, as they had planned. Since they had plenty of time, Meredith suggested going to the slightly upscale restaurant, Abbey's Grill, which had an excellent menu and simple but elegant décor. Evan drove them there in his black Jeep Cherokee. He insisted on opening the door to the jeep for her as she was ready to get in, which made her smile inside.

After entering the restaurant and sitting down at their table near a large palm tree, Evan smiled at her with his steel blue eyes, looking intelligent but playful.

"Now, tell me, Dr. Mason, how did you become the staring soloist for the Philharmonic after only being here for six months?"

Without trying to brag or go on endlessly, Meredith told him about her education, her scholarships, the long list of competitions she had won, and the major US cities whose symphonies she had already played with. She tried to explain how none of that was really important to her and how the only thing that really mattered was the playing and sharing of her music. Without trying to sound conceited, she went on and tried to explain how her playing touched the innermost part of her being and how sharing that part of herself through performing brought deep fulfillment to her. She told him she had an agent and that she hoped she would start getting perform-ing engagements in other cities again.

"Wow, that's incredibly impressive! I'm almost embarrassed to share my meager credentials with you after hearing that! Maybe I ought to slide down in my seat and slip out the back door while I can still escape," chided Evan.

"No, really, I want to know all about you," said Meredith seri-ously. "I'm really not the cultural snob I might appear to be."

"No, you are quite the opposite." He smiled sincerely. "I actu-ally am on the math faculty at UNC Asheville. I teach calculus." Meredith rolled her eyes in amazement.

"Oh my. I've heard that mathematicians who are good at music are very brilliant people."

"I don't know about that." Evan laughed. "I actually minored in music in college and was always first cello in the university sym-phony. I just wanted to pursue math as a career choice."

Meredith commented on how many brilliant physicians and very successful people in other careers were often outstanding musi-cians. Evan said he had a few private students in Asheville and that he enjoyed teaching them as a relaxing change to his normal job. Dr. Preston found him through a recommendation from the conductor of the Asheville symphony, with which he played first cello. They began chatting about Asheville and what a unique little mountain town it was, drawing an array of artists and craftsmen to the area. He promised to take her there sometime soon.

The smells of shrimp and grits, jambalaya, and homemade soups filled the air, making them hungrier by the minute. Their food came, and it was exceptionally delicious. Meredith had the shrimp and grits, and Evan had the Southern fried chicken with mashed potatoes. Sharing a pot of steaming tea turned out to be the perfect ending to their first time out together.

After spending more time at the restaurant than they should have, they got back to the college just in time for Meredith's faculty meeting and Evan's symphony block. Evan had insisted on picking up the check at the restaurant, which gave Meredith a sweet feeling inside as she watched him hurry down the hall to make his rehearsal.

He had been warm and friendly, and Meredith had enjoyed sharing her feelings about her music with him. Being a musician himself, he seemed to understand all her deep feelings about her craft.

Having a friend would be nice. Very nice!

6

Music gives a soul to the universe, wings to the mind, flight
to the imagination, and life to everything.

—Plato

Meredith practiced intensely, almost feverishly, for the rest of the
week and on into the weekend. Her playing freed her spirit like the
wind capturing a balloon filled with helium and letting it fly free in
the breeze. She felt like a bird in flight, able to see from one edge of
the horizon to the other. The enjoyment that filled her was the essence
of life itself sprinkled about in sound flowing wildly and unencumbered throughout the room. Pleased with how the Rachmaninoff
was sounding, she decided to call it a day. Saturday evening made it
reason enough not to have to fix a meal for herself, so she picked up
some takeout and went home to crash for the rest of the weekend.

As she sat down to eat, the phone rang. Surprise and a sense of
pleasure filled her upon realizing that it was Evan Sanders calling. He
thanked her for sharing the nice lunch with him on Wednesday and
said how much he had enjoyed getting to know her, even if only for a
short midweek lunch. Commenting that both their schedules would
become more full as the date for the Rachmaninoff approached, he
admitted regret that his living and teaching in Asheville got in the
way of his seeing her more often, but he wanted her to know how
much he had enjoyed her company and how talented he realized she
was. She sat smiling as she hung up, having savored each compliment
as it was given, realizing how sweet he was and how nice it was to
have met him.

Dr. Preston assigned cello sectionals to Evan for his supervi-
sion for the next few weeks. Meredith was happily settled into her

new teaching schedule, busy teaching by day and practicing for the Rachmaninoff in the late afternoons and evenings. Two weeks had gone by, and she only passed Evan in the halls on a few occasions but rarely got to say more than a few words to him. Things were progressing nicely musically. She was scheduled to play with the full symphony on Saturday morning, one week before the scheduled concert.

Saturday morning arrived. The symphony setup was on the stage in Twitchell auditorium, where the concert would be held. The large Steinway was sitting center stage, with its high gloss gleaming, waiting for Meredith's magic touch. Recently restored to its original splendor, Twitchell was an amazing hall, with exceptional acoustics. Performing halls built today just did not measure up sound-wise to what had been built in the past. This one was a gem. The high newly painted white archways of the tremendous ceiling allowed the sound from the stage to resonate perfectly, creating delight for the listening ear. Rows and rows of scarlet velvet-covered seats sat clean and empty, waiting to be filled by the first audience of the season. The normally open orchestra pit was closed, and the symphony would sit upon the old wooden floor of the stage in chairs, so they could be seen by the audience.

Nine forty-five a.m. saw the students and professionals unpacking their instruments, tuning, and quietly chatting with one another. Evan gave Meredith a wink from the front of the cello section. She smiled back as she relaxed her body and adjusted the height of her padded piano bench. Dr. Preston's plan was to run the first movement all the way through, including all of Meredith's parts so the students could become used to hearing them. She sat quietly, boosting her concentration so she could do her best.

Meredith composed herself at the piano, mentally getting ready to perform. After working for two hours in her studio prior to the rehearsal, she felt ready to tackle the adventure that was about to begin. Two hours of practice would have tired a normal person. Two hours of practice put Meredith in prime form, ready to begin with energy. It would be an adventure, an adventure pulling together her musical skills, her concentration, and her creative ability to mold the orchestra into a oneness that would follow her and capture the essence of the piece Rachmaninoff had created. The piece would begin with solo piano. Meredith would begin the concerto alone, set the tempo, and create the opening mood. Dr. Preston raised his baton, getting the full attention of the orchestra. He nodded to Meredith that they were ready.

The piece was in a minor key and would begin with a pensive, somber mood. She began quietly with a series of bell-like chords echoed by octaves in the bass that would crescendo and build tension one after another until they climaxed with the introduction of the main theme by the strings. Then she began a series of rolling minor arpeggios that created an undercurrent of sound supporting the beauty of the string section. The strings came in with a sweet but sad, haunting melody that was intense and Russian in sound, singing the melody with the somberness and eerie quality Meredith had helped create as she supported them. Meredith playfully ran her fingers over the keyboard in a series of treble runs and then came in with the second theme.

The piece brought to mind a cold, chilling image of grayness. A mirage of darkness, depression, heaviness, and struggle came to mind as one listened to the spooky melody floating through the air like wispy ghosts flying through the night.

Meredith's part teased the cellos, trading the melody back and forth with them, followed by the piano singing forth, as the woodwinds entered. Meredith totally gave herself to the music, taunting each section of the orchestra that came in to playfully bounce back and forth with her. A French horn solo came in sadly and serenely with the melody, followed by the piano and strings echoing the sadness, crying forth with tears of melancholy. Piano runs accompanied the crying of the strings, just before the movement finished with full orchestra creating an agitated coda, with the piano playing forcefully, somberly, and triumphantly, with an energetic minor chord finish.

At the end of the movement, after a quick "bravo," Dr. Preston began with several corrections he wanted to implement. Evan could hardly pay attention to Dr. Preston and what he was saying. He stared at Meredith's statuesque small frame sitting at the piano, her luminous large brown eyes wide open, taking in all that was going on.

He had been mesmerized by the emotion and intensity with which she played, having trouble concentrating on his own part, as he got caught up in the web of her playing. The melodies had sung out from her heart and her soul. Loosing herself in the music, the amazing feat was that she drew in the rest of the players to become one with the music and with her. Evan was totally taken with Meredith and with her ability to create the mood she molded. He felt like he had just been a part of some great whole, which he had. It was an experience, not just the rehearsal of some notes. He felt great admiration for Meredith, for her devotion to her music, and for what she had accomplished. He sat staring at her, noticing how very beautiful she was, sitting there in angelic fashion, quietly listening to what was going on between Dr. Preston and the orchestra.

"Cellos. Measure 96 please. Mr. Sanders, measure 96." Dr. Preston gave Evan an impatient look. Evan was embarrassed that Dr. Preston had picked up on his fascination with Meredith's playing. He hoped his fascination with Meredith herself had not been as obvious.

The rehearsal went well, although all were exhausted at its conclusion. Dr. Preston had pressed them hard and had kept his stern work ethic throughout the rehearsal. Moments of gentle praise were there, but basically, his strong correction presided to draw out what he knew was musically possible from this group.

As soon as he dismissed the orchestra, Dr. Preston came to Meredith's side. Giving her a great big bear hug, he gave the ultimate compliment. "You were fabulous! Your playing was intense. The orchestra followed your lead and instantly became part of the mood you created for them. Today was the best I have heard them play this piece, ever, and that is no lie! I knew you were the perfect pianist to pull this all together! Bravo!" He gave her another hug, and took pride in her the way a father would take pride in a daughter he had nurtured through the years, although he had worked with Meredith for only a short time. Meredith smiled and knew the rehearsal had gone extremely well even before Dr. Preston had said anything. She had felt it too. They spoke briefly about the timing of some entrances, followed by Dr. Preston quickly excusing himself, as he was off to another meeting.

Most of the students and professionals had left when Evan quietly made his way up to the piano, where Meredith was organizing her music. He slowly walked up beside her and just stared, quietly at first, before he spoke.

"You were incredible. There's no other word for it. You probably have no idea on the effect you just had on everyone. You began playing, and you wove a spell that took every player with you. We all experienced it. It was a thrilling ride with everyone following your lead! It was magic!"

Meredith just stared quietly back at him. She was used to the compliments, and she usually barely heard them. She didn't play for the compliments. She was studying Evan, noticing how the dimples in his cheeks got larger as he spoke more emphatically and how the few golden sprigs at the front of his hair bounced down on his face the more animated he got. She just smiled back at him. This was who she was. This was how her playing affected people. This was how she enjoyed the gift that had been given to her at birth and developed by years and years of hard work.

Evan apologized and then began to ramble unceasingly.

"Listen. I've got to go back to Asheville for my evening class, but you've got to promise me something. Come to Asheville for the day on Sunday with me! I could give you a royal tour. We could get some fantastic food and see the leaves at their peak color. And we could get to know each other a little better. What do you say, will you come? I won't take no for an answer! I could pick you up at home and everything! You'll love Asheville! You have to come! It will be a good break for you from all of your hard work. You need to come. What do you say!"

Meredith smiled, wondering if he would ever stop, or if he would even take no for an answer! She knew she needed a break. It would be good for her, and she really did want to get to know Evan better. She barely ever got to talk to him. Fighting her perfectionist urge to spend the whole weekend practicing, her mind and heart gave in to her desire to have more fun and get to know Evan a little better.

"Well, I'll probably make you late for your class if I don't agree to come right now, and I wouldn't want to do that!" She laughed. Evan hurriedly began gathering up his belongings.

"Fantastic. I'll pick you up at ten o'clock. Wear blue jeans and a warm sweater. It's ten degrees colder up there in the mountains," shouted Evan as he began running toward the door.

"Yes, sir," replied Meredith dutifully. With that, he flew out of the door and was gone. Her heart fluttered a bit as she watched him go. He was sweet and gentle and kind.

Her thoughts left Evan for a moment, and she thought about what she had just accomplished at her first rehearsal with the symphony here in Spartanburg. She stood for a long time and stared at the performing hall, now empty and void of all noise. It had a presence of its own. All concert halls did, especially when they were empty. She stood and soaked in the experience in silence. She felt connected to this hall now. It would become a part of her. It held a long history of those who had performed there before her, and now she would be a part of that history too. She wondered about those who had performed here in the past and about those who were still to come in the future. She left quietly, feeling that all was right in her life at this point in time and space.

Meredith stopped at the grocery store on her way home and bought the ingredients to make chocolate chip cookies. There was a recipe on the back of the package of chips, and she made sure that she had put everything she needed for the project in her cart before she made her way to the checkout. She even purchased two cookie sheets and a mixing bowl since she really didn't think she had any baking utensils at home. She hadn't baked in years and really didn't do much cooking. Somehow the idea of going to the mountains with Evan made her feel domestic for some reason she didn't understand. She just knew she wanted to bake cookies.

Upon arriving home, she began her project. Before long, the wonderful smell of chocolate was floating through her house. How yummy something as simple as a chocolate chip cookie could smell! And how special making a cookie for someone special could make you feel!

That night at ten, Meredith's phone rang.

"Good evening," said Evan, trying to sound mysterious like Alfred Hitchcock.

"I just realized that I have no idea where you live!"

"That's right! You don't." Meredith laughed.

"I would have been waiting here on the sidewalk all morning, wouldn't I?"

"Well, not *all* morning," teased Evan. She gave him the easy directions to her house from the college and told him he should have no trouble finding it.

Again, he told her how impressed he was with her playing and how she had held the whole orchestra captive with her powers. She thanked him kindly and said she had not intended to take any prisoners. It was Evan who was laughing as they hung up, thinking of Meredith with her tiny, slim frame taking prisoners for ransom. He was looking forward to tomorrow. And so was she.

7

Music washes away from the soul the dust
of everyday life.
—Berthold Auerbach

And so would a play day in the mountains! The music would come with them in their souls, as a sense of frivolity and newness of spirit was created as a fresh relationship was being born.

Meredith was dressed and ready at nine forty-five Sunday morning, wearing blue jeans, a long-sleeved camel sweater, and a pair of suede sneakers. She thought she'd carry her thigh-length scarlet-red hooded sweater just in case it really was ten degrees colder in Asheville. She also carried some scarlet-red wool mittens to protect her hands and fingers from the cold. The sun was beaming brightly outside, and the day promised to be a gorgeous one.

Meredith answered the knock at her door at 10:00 a.m. Evan looked approvingly at Meredith.

"Hey. You look really nice," he said, sincerely meaning it.

"Thank you." Meredith smiled. He was staring at her, admiring her huge brown eyes and silky long brown hair. She became conscious of him watching her and then nervously chimed in with, "I made some chocolate chip cookies for us to take." Evan kept looking at her with his steel-blue eyes, conscious that he had perhaps thrown her off guard with his stares.

"I can't believe the woman bakes too! Is there anything you *can't* do?" he replied. "How about if I just sample one to make sure they're suitable for our journey?" Meredith opened the cookie tin. Evan reached for one and stole a second as Meredith pretended to slap his hand in protest.

"I'll carry the cookies," proclaimed Meredith. Evan pretended to look wounded as Meredith locked up the house. He walked her to the passenger side of the jeep and opened the door for her. She was tickled because it had been years since anyone had done that for her. She was a bit old-fashioned herself and appreciated that quality in him she had noticed the other day as well. It was a kind of sweetness that a lot of guys seemed to lack today.

After they started down the road, she couldn't resist teasing him about his Carolina *hey*.

"Now, explain to me the logic behind this *hey* word," said Meredith. "In New York, when you see someone on the street, you say hi. Hay is for horses. No one would have any idea what I meant if I greeted them with some 'hay.'" She laughed.

"Well, you've just discovered my Southern origins," confessed Evan. "I'm Southern born and bred. The word *hey* is standard fare down here. There are a whole bunch of words like that that every-one just assumes are normal words in the English language. Like *mash*. You don't *press* a button down South, you *mash* the button. Everyone knows what you mean. Another one is *y'all*. *Y'all* is a way to include everyone, which Southerners are very good at doing. It's plural. Now you on the other hand, '*waulking* the *dawg*,' 'drinking *wawter*' and eating '*hot dawgs*,' you have to admit, is pretty strange." He was enjoying razing her back. Meredith smiled.

"I've really enjoyed the friendliness since I've come down South. The pace of life is just slower, and it feels more comfortable, even though y'all tawk funny down here!"

"Ah, I can see a new Southerner being born right before my very eyes," chided Evan.

They drove through Spartanburg and got on I-26, heading for the North Carolina border. The reds and oranges and yellows of the leaves became more pronounced as they drove further to the North. There was just enough green still left on some of the trees to mix in splendidly with the colors.

"This is the area of South Carolina known as the Piedmont, which means foothills," began Evan. "We're about to cross into North Carolina. Little historic towns like Saluda and Tryon are sprinkled throughout this area. This is apple-growing country! Maybe we can even pick up a jug of cider on the way home to go with your cookies!" Meredith noticed that the road began to wind upward and that the hill began to look like a small mountain.

"This is the Saluda grade," continued Evan. "When we near the top, you can turn your head around and take in the expansive view. The temperature will drop as we climb the grade. In the summertime, the humidity drops as well. This is the land of waterfalls and some pretty nice camping areas." Meredith was enjoying the view and the lecture about the area as well. More fir trees began to mix with the hardwoods as they continued upward. The view was amazing. It was almost like being in an airplane.

They drove through a retirement area known as Hendersonville and began seeing signs for the Asheville airport and other landmarks for Asheville.

"We'll be going near a historic home known as the Biltmore house. George Vanderbilt built the mansion back in 1895. It rivals some of the castles and mansions in Europe and is currently open as a tourist attraction. We won't have time to visit it today, but we'll definitely come back. At Christmastime, there is a tree in each of the many rooms and the decorations are stunning."

Meredith smiled at how *they* had suddenly become a *we* and how he took for granted that their relationship would continue on to Christmas and beyond. The way he talked made her feel secure and comfortable. She hadn't had anyone in her life like Evan. She was pleased with how their relationship was going and with how relaxed she felt with him. He was sweet and kind and definitely handsome. He treated her like a lady, and she felt extremely happy every time she had been with him.

As they made the turn onto I-40, Meredith could see the buildings of downtown Asheville.

"Now remember, Asheville is a little town, but it has a quaint personality that is all its own. The more time you spend here, the more endearing it becomes. We'll find a place to park and then go exploring. Deciding where to eat lunch will be the difficult part! The restaurants are numerous, and the food is well worth the drive up here!"

Evan found a place to park, and they both got out, but not before Evan attacked the cookies again. This time Meredith let him eat his fill and called him the cookie monster.

The sidewalk was a hill. It went upward, and in places, had lumpy cracked concrete. Evan stopped, smiled, looked down at her, and put out his hand. "I wouldn't want my lady to tumble," he said. Meredith smiled up at him and held out her hand. Evan took it and gently cupped his other hand over the top of hers just for a moment. "These are precious hands. We have to protect them for the big concert next week." He stood still for a moment longer, holding her hand with both of his, looking into her beautiful brown eyes with admiration. They were both obviously enjoying the hand-holding. Then they continued up the hill, hand in hand, passing a few shops, a wine store, and a bakery that smelled heavenly! "I'm thinking we should have lunch now so we'll have lots of time to explore the shops afterward. Then we'll have time for a nice dinner before we head back. There's a really nice old-fashioned café at the top of this hill, with food to die for," said Evan.

"Sounds great," remarked Meredith.

They walked into the Bistro 1896 at the top of the hill, which faced Pack Square, and looked out on part of the town and part of the mountains in the background. The bright reds and oranges and yellows of the leaves painted a magnificent background for the skyline of the city. The air was crisp and had a slight chill that was not present in Spartanburg. There was patio seating, but they asked for a table inside by the window to keep Meredith's hands warm and soak in the rays of the sun. She told Evan she had brought woolen gloves for later if it got cold.

The restaurant was old but had a charm all its own. Old-fashioned chairs and tables sat on old but polished hardwood floors. An array of pictures and posters filled the walls.

The menu presented a challenge, for neither of them could decide what to select. Meredith finally ordered chipotle cheddar shrimp and grits, mixed with red peppers and gorgonzola sauce.

Evan chose a dish of shrimp, andouille sausage, roasted red peppers, and spinach, topped with a Cajun cream sauce served over polenta. Meredith commented that they might not have room for dinner after feasting on this lunch, but Evan said it was only eleven thirty, and that surely they could walk it off by dinnertime, with all of these hills in the sidewalks!

Evan took Meredith's hands over the table, looked at her in the eyes, and rubbed her fingers with his thumbs. After not saying anything for a moment, he blurted out, "I'd like to get to know you better. You've just overwhelmed me…your talent, your sensitive nature, your innocent way of looking at the world even though you have already achieved so much…everything about you. You are sweet and sincere, and all I've seemed to be able to do is bump into you as I'm rushing off somewhere else to do something I'd prefer not to be doing at the moment. I know I must seem self-centered and uncaring." She looked back at him sweetly.

"You don't seem that way at all. I'd like to get to know you better too. You've been the handsome cellist in the first row of the symphony who stares at me when he should be playing his part, and all I've been able to say is goodbye before he charges out the door."

"I know," said Evan, almost embarrassed that she had caught him staring at her in practice and that his schedule never left him time to talk with her very much.

Evan looked at her again, noticing the innocence and inquisitiveness her eyes revealed.

"Tell me about yourself. Where did you grow up?"

"I grew up in northern New Jersey. Yes, I'm a Yankee in Southern territory! I was an only child, and my parents doted on me, since I was the only one. I never really had anyone to talk to. I was quiet, and I was a loner. So I dove into my activities full force. I was given ballet and tap lessons, and I grew to love classical music through my dancing. I danced to the beautiful music, as it set my soul on fire. But then I realized I could make the beautiful music myself. I began studying the piano, and the lessons touched my heart in a special way when I was only in the second grade. I would come home from school and spend the whole afternoon getting lost in the beauty of my music. I was playing stuff far too advanced for anyone my age. My parents realized that and found me a really excellent teacher, who acknowledged my potential and helped me to advance rapidly. He gave me a firm foundation in theory and technique, and I just blossomed. I practiced religiously every day. We lived in a rural area, and my music was what I cherished and loved. I really didn't have any children to play with after school since we lived far out from the town. I did well in my studies, but my music was what I treasured. I don't know if I can tell you this next chapter of my life without getting emotional." She paused, looking down at the table, wanting to be honest but not wanting to have to tell the tale.

"No, please, go on. I want to know all about you. Even the painful parts of your life."

"Well, this is more than painful. No one should have to have gone through anything like this." Again she paused, not really wanting to share this part of herself. "I don't think I've ever told this to anyone before, that is, anyone who did not live through it with me."

"Go on. Please. You can trust me."

"It's not about trust, it's about…" she stopped, not knowing how to say everything. "No, I can't. I'm sorry but I just can't. There's too much hurt there. I just don't think I'm ready to share it yet. I've never told anyone. I just don't think I can right now. I'm sorry." Tears welled up in her beautiful brown eyes, and she was struggling hard not to let the flood gates down and let all the pent-up emotion come pouring out.

"It's okay. It's really okay. You don't have to tell me if it's too painful. I understand. I really do."

Tears started running down Meredith's face. She tried to wipe them away, but the more she tried, the more they streamed down her face. She had never come this close to sharing her hurt with anyone. And she was embarrassed that she was crying in front of this gentle, sweet man who seemed to honestly care.

Evan took her hands again as he looked at her, not knowing how to comfort her or help her through this moment of obvious pain. "I know I can't say anything to lesson your pain. But I can be here for you. And if at some time you are ready to share it with me, I would be honored for you to do that."

Meredith looked up at this sweet, thoughtful man who was sitting here, listening to her pour her heart out. And he wanted to share her pain. That was kind of incredible. After just sitting for a long time, she composed herself and went on.

"Life wasn't the same after what had happened. I poured my sorrow into my music every day. It was my therapy. I played my heart out. It was what got me through that horrible time. Things were never quite the same. Even the music couldn't totally fill the hole inside my soul."

"But when you are ready, I am here for you. Sometimes sharing something with another person helps." Evan didn't know what else to say at the moment. Meredith went on.

"My music has been everything to me. It's really all that I have…everything that's important to me." She stopped pouring out her heart and looked at her fingers as Evan was still rubbing them with his thumbs. Evan looked down.

"I'm sorry for all you've been through," he confided. Meredith smiled.

"Life is good now, and I have much to be thankful for."

Evan paused and then said, "Yes…but in a way you are like me."

Looking puzzled, she said, "What do you mean?" She looked up at him with unsure eyes. He looked back at her cautiously, knowing that he had had no right to say what he was about to say and that he was stepping on shaky ground, but he made his comment anyway. His steely blue eyes met her large brown eyes and held her gaze for what seemed like an eternity.

"We both have no one to share everything with." There. It was said, and he knew it was true. They were both alone despite the interesting lives they led. He felt a great attraction to Meredith. He yearned to grow closer to her and to know her. Meredith held her head down.

"Yes." She sat for a moment and then said, "Now tell me about your life." She slowly pulled her hands back into her lap and looked into his eyes once again, not knowing how much trust she could put in this new relationship. "Doesn't someone as attractive as you have a girlfriend or a past girlfriend?" And then she started ranting. "You just flew into Spartanburg, into my life, and I know nothing at all about you except that you are terrifically handsome, teach math, and play the cello, and that Dr. Prentice, whom I greatly respect, likes you and your work very much. You could be an ax murderer for all I know and who knows what else," she said with a bit of amusement in her voice. And then she calmed down for a bit, gently adding, "But I know that you live in this charming place called Asheville, which you so kindly wanted to share with me today, and that feels very good."

Evan took a deep breath. "Well, where do I start?" he began. "No, I'm not an ax murderer, so you don't have to concern yourself about that. Do I have a girlfriend? No, there is no girlfriend. I came to Asheville several years ago when I got my teaching job and fell in love with the area…the snow in the winter, the beautiful fall and spring weather, the musical excitement of the festivals in the town. Most of the women I meet are the young, giggling, miniskirted university coeds, who really don't know how to relate to someone like me or have anything in common with me. They may be attracted to me, but I usually try to run the other way. They are pretty on the outside, but most of them seem to have no substance on the inside. Many of them flunk out after a year because they don't try, and most of them are unsure of who they are and what they want and are just here for a year or two before they move on to a full university instead of a branch. Then there are the older hippie women who smoke pot, the artists who are also trying to find themselves, the women with tattoos covering half of their bodies—or even all of their bodies—and the older retirees who come to the area for the weather and the sheer beauty of the place. There is no one special here for me. Really. It's a quiet, peaceful, satisfying life but a bit of a lonely one. I graduated from UNC in Chapel Hill with a double major in math and music. Math and music both came easy to me, and I really didn't have to work hard to do well in either of them. I was the typical pretty-faced frat boy, who got drunk on weekends and basically just had fun without feeling much responsibility for my future. I brought someone different to the fraternity parties each weekend and didn't think much about it. I did date someone for six months during my senior year. I began to think maybe she was someone I could begin to build a relationship with. She was a pretty sorority girl, someone who made me look good having her on my arm. And then I found out she was dating someone else at the same time she was dating me and that she was just as shallow as I had been. An experience like that shoots you way down. And it hurt. I dropped her like a hot potato and didn't care to get serious with anyone after that. I just floated through the rest of my college experience, never really facing the need to think about the future.

"My parents had put me through the university and through grad school without really being very involved in my life except paying for it. I was an only child, so there was no brother or sister to help create a sense of family. I rarely saw them during my college years, and then all of a sudden, they decided they wanted to retire in Northern California. My father was tired of his life as an engineer and wanted to move on. They just left without even much of a goodbye. I see them maybe once a year. They're really not interested in me or what I'm doing," said Evan. Meredith looked back with understanding.

"That must be painful too."

"It is," said Evan, "but I've accepted it and thrive on my teaching and being involved with my music. I play with the Asheville Symphony, and that brings me just a little bit of what your music brings you. So I've been peacefully living this mundane life, until I stuck my head into your studio door and met this incredibly beautiful and talented creature who seems to be perfect in every way. You've thrown me a bit off balance… I didn't expect to bump into someone like you who would begin to occupy my every thought." Meredith didn't know what to say. She just sat quietly for a moment.

Fortunately, their food came, and they leaned back as the waiter put down the steaming plates.

"We'll have two sweet teas," said Evan to the waiter. After he left, Evan said, "I just know that you are a Southern girl now as far as the tea goes. You are, right?"

"You guessed it." Meredith smiled.

The food was incredible. They savored every bite and left the complicated issues behind as they ate. Meredith just looked at Evan every now and then, hoping that he was the kind, sweet person she saw as they talked. She had not been in a serious relationship before and yearned to have someone to trust and confide in. She had occasionally, very occasionally, dated some real jerks for a while, while she was in New York. That experience just made her not even care to search for someone she could have a genuine, meaningful relationship with. Was it better to be alone and have life be gentle but lonely as hell, or was it better to take the chance of being hurt again and hope that what you saw on the outside of a person was truly what was on the inside? She hoped the latter was true. She so hoped that it was true.

Evan stole quick looks at Meredith while she was busy eating. He saw an incredibly sweet, intelligent, sincere person who was quite beautiful, with her long shiny brown hair, huge brown eyes, and slender, delicate figure. She had a way about her that just made him happy to be with her, even if they weren't talking. Somehow it just felt right. He felt like he had found the four-leaf clover in the clover patch. Without so much as searching, he had stumbled upon a rare diamond, a precious jewel of a woman. Did she look at him in the same way? Was he someone special to her, or was he just someone to eat lunch with? He didn't know. He hoped she was beginning to feel about him the way he was feeling about her.

"Dessert?" the waiter asked, interrupting both of their thoughts. "Oh my goodness, no way," Meredith answered. "I think I would explode! The food was wonderful!"

"Good," Evan said. This is one of my most favorite places to eat. It's not fancy, but you can't beat the food!" Evan grabbed the check, and they both left full, looking forward to the afternoon.

"Thanks," Meredith said. "I really needed that. I've been a little tense with the concert coming up, and this was the perfect antidote." Evan smiled and put his hand on her shoulder as they walked out the door.

"I'm glad we came too," he said.

There was a whole array of assorted shops and galleries to explore and visit. Some were antique shops, some were stores displaying artwork, and some were just little boutique stores with unique gift items for sale. There were more restaurants, candy shops, and bakeries. Evan took her hand as they walked. "Now remember," I'm responsible for the safety of these hands this weekend," he said as he patted the hand he held with his other.

"Oh, is that what it is," she said, smiling. He squeezed her hand and smiled at her as they continued on.

The smell of freshly made peanut brittle lured them into a small candy shop, which was also filled with all kinds of homemade chocolates and marzipan candies.

"I think I'll die if I don't have some of this peanut brittle," Evan said. After ordering a pound, he asked Meredith what she would like. She ordered a pound of chocolates filled with lemon, strawberry, and raspberry buttercream filling. As they each munched on their bag of goodies, Meredith remarked that she would hold Evan totally responsible if her concert gown did not fit next weekend.

"Now there's no way someone like you could take on the shape of the Pillsbury dough girl by next weekend," he said, defending his decadent purchase.

"I don't know," she laughed, cramming one of each flavor of the chocolates into her mouth.

"I'll tell Dr. Preston it's all your fault when I have to wear one of the school-choir robes to perform in instead of my slender ball gown."

"Well, if that's the case," Evan remarked playfully, "I'll just have to dispose of the evidence." He playfully grabbed Meredith's bag of chocolates and began running down the street with it. He ducked behind trash cans, large bushes, and into alleys as Meredith got into the spirit of the chase to repossess her bag of chocolates. Tourists walking slowly looked at them strangely, but they continued on like two children playing a game, chasing and dodging each other with a silly mindset. She followed him down a small alley and jumped as be bounced out at her, scaring her out of her wits as she let out a scream. Grabbing the bag from his hand, she pulled out another three chocolates, smirked at him, and stuffed them into her mouth. The chase was over. They sat down on a bench, not knowing whether it was the sweetness of the game or the sweetness of the candy that made them laugh like two seven-year-olds.

Evan looked about and then made an executive decision. "I think we need to go back to the car now." Being the perfect tour guide, he didn't want her to miss anything. "I'd like to drive down I-240 so you can see the Smokies looking west. The Asheville mountains are special. They have a quality unique to this area. And besides, if we go back to the car, I can attack the cookies again now that we've walked off that lunch and have had our little candy jog.

"Oh, I see the real reasoning behind this ploy," she teased. After getting in the car, Meredith snacked on a cookie with Evan. It was already four thirty, and lunchtime had passed a long time ago. They turned onto the interstate, and after driving for a while past a motley assortment of strip malls and car dealerships, they rounded a corner and the beauty of the Tennessee Smokies was suddenly before them.

"You're right," said Meredith, taking in the beautiful scenery with her mouth practically open. "They are different from other mountains!"

"Of course I'm right," said Evan, defending himself. "They're absolutely stunning in a way that is different from other mountain ranges in this part of the country." Meredith studied them with much thought. They looked like lumps of cookie dough that began to melt together when plopped on a pan that was put in the oven. Behind the plops of mountains, the sky glowed with the purples and oranges and pinks surrounding the setting sun, looking as if pastel watercolor had been applied with a brush. The mountains appeared to be rolling in layers, followed by forests of colored trees below. Then the car would round a corner, and all of a sudden, tall peaks would appear like ocean waves ready to break on the road. On the way back, puffs of white billowy clouds looked like scattered balls of cotton thrown upon the intensity of the blue sky. Meredith rode quietly for a while, stunned by the scenery, contemplating how perfect the day had been and how much she had enjoyed being with Evan. Evan seemed to pick up on her thoughts, as he rode quietly too, enjoying the peaceful serene feeling they shared between themselves, and the memories of the silliness that seemed to have bound them together.

"I have a special place for dinner," Evan revealed. "Do you like Mediterranean food? We'll have to drive back downtown again, but we have to go back that way anyway to get home, and if you like Mediterranean, you'll love the food in this place!"

"I haven't had Mediterranean in ages," Meredith confessed, "but I do love it."

"Well then, we're off to the Mediterranean Garden Café. And if it wasn't a Sunday evening, we would be able to have a belly dancer perform during our dinner." Evan laughed. Meredith looked at him unbelievably.

"Oh come on now, you're not serious."

"Perfectly serious," howled Evan. "You're really missing a thrilling experience, but there's always next time, my dear!" Meredith howled out loud, imagining a belly dancer weaving around their table, wiggling her body parts to the intriguing music. She wondered what kind of place he was taking her to, but she decided it was best to just sit back and enjoy the adventure.

The bright fuchsia pink, gold, and blue walls of the Mediterranean Garden Café jumped out at them as they were led to their little round rattan table. Wonderful smells of Morocco, Lebanon, Turkey, and Egypt floated around the room as they sat down.

"If I were a dog, I think I'd be salivating by now," joked Evan as they surveyed the delightful menu the waitress brought them. "I think we should order two dishes and share them…a vegetarian platter and maybe a chicken dish. How does that sound?"

"Tantalizing," replied Meredith. The vegetarian dish Evan chose for them came with hummus, hot pita, baba ghanoush, tahini salad, tabbouleh, olives, falafel, and stuffed grape leaves. Evan selected a Jordanian marinated and grilled chicken dish for their meat platter. Meredith confessed that she only knew half of the items they ordered but that she trusted Evan explicitly. He was pleased that she put her faith in him. When the food came, Evan and Meredith devoured every bit of it. They had baklava and Turkish coffee for dessert and were barely able to walk out of the restaurant they were so full.

"The Pillsbury dough girl strikes again," Evan teased as he put his arm around Meredith. They walked back to the car, talking about the unusual foods they had just enjoyed and giggled about the belly dancer they would have seen if it had been a Saturday night. Evan tried to do a demonstration of the belly dancing but agreed that was not his talent.

Dusk was setting in, and the ride back to Spartanburg would be in darkness lit only by the light of the stars. Evan opened Meredith's door for her and then got in on his own side. Before starting the car, he sat quietly, just looking at her for a moment, and she at him.

"I want you to know I had a wonderful time today," Evan said honestly and sincerely. I can't remember a day like this…ever."

"Me too," Meredith replied shyly.

"And Meredith, I meant every bit of what I said in the restaurant earlier today. You are an amazing woman, and the fact that you've come into my life…is just so very special."

"Thank you," she said, meaning it with all sincerity. He took her hand and kissed it softly, holding it for a moment before starting the ignition. They rode quietly for a long time, each thinking about the other.

The ride down the Saluda Grade was lit by the light of the stars. It was as if the whole universe shone above them.

"We'll have to come up here some night and search for constellations," Evan said. "It's so dark out here at night that you can see them really well. I can find them from all the sky searching that I did during my Boy Scout days," he bragged. Meredith thought of the image of Evan dressed in a Boy Scout uniform and giggled to herself.

"It would be delightful having my own Boy Scout for a guide."

"My pleasure," Evan responded. Meredith could tell that he was smiling as he said this even though she couldn't see his face in the darkness.

They pulled up in front of Meredith's house on Palmetto Street. Evan got out first, walked around the Jeep, and opened the car door for her. He reached for her hand and walked slowly beside her, stopping at the bottom of the stairs to take a falling leaf out of her hair. He cupped his hands softly on her cheeks and gently leaned forward, kissing her ever so tenderly on the lips. Meredith closed her eyes and enjoyed the gentleness of his touch, feeling a warm exciting rush move upward through her body. She opened her eyes, and he was looking into them, stroking her hair and enjoying the beauty of the angelic face that stared into his eyes. He leaned toward her again, this time putting his arms around her, pulling her close to him with another kiss as she enjoyed his embrace at last. It was the touch she hadn't realized that she had longed for.

The moon shone through the leaves of the tall trees as he leaned back again, holding her by the shoulders and staring into the face he had recently come to adore.

"I'm going to go," Evan said. "If I don't leave now, I won't want to go at all." He cupped her face and ever so softly kissed her on the forehead. Holding her hand, he led her up the stairway and stood by her side as she opened her door.

"Good night," he said as he waived and walked down the stairs back to the car. Meredith said nothing and just waived, mesmerized by the feelings that stirred within her.

The next morning at nine o'clock, Meredith's phone rang in her studio as she was getting ready to begin a lesson.

"Hi," said the voice on the other end.

"Hi."

"Do you have a lesson now?" Evan asked.

"Yes."

"Well, shoot!"

"My thoughts exactly!"

He paused and then sincerely said, "It was an incredibly special day yesterday for me. I just wanted you to know."

"I know. I thought it was too!"

"Good! I'll see you tonight amidst the beginning noise and commotion of the rehearsal, and I'll give you a wink, if nothing else!"

"Okay," she beamed. "Bye!"

"Bye."

She could tell he was grinning on the other end of the phone.

8

We are the music makers. And we are the dreamers of dreams.

—Arthur O'Shaughnessy

The entire symphony, largely made up of professionals, was due to rehearse Monday through Friday this week at seven in preparation for Saturday's concert. The excitement would build as the end of the week drew nearer. Meredith was very excited and very ready for the week to begin. Dr. Preston would be stern and demanding, but he would draw the very best out of the entire group. It was all about the finished product in the end. The concert was sold out already, and the audience would be made up of the musically-in-the-know people of the area.

Rehearsals went well all week long. Meredith barely got to speak with Evan at all and only briefly at the end of each rehearsal. He had suggested they go out for coffee after the first rehearsal, but she declined. She said he had to drive back to Asheville. She was always very strict with herself the week before a concert, taking her rest ahead of any other commitments so she would do well in performance. He said he understood and gave her a gentle peck on the cheek each night as he left her. He called each night after he got home, telling her how much he wished the circumstances were different. She agreed. They discussed the rehearsals. The performance as a whole got better and better as the week went on, if that was possible.

Dr. Preston, despite his stern demeanor during rehearsals, was extremely pleased with everything and piled the praise on Meredith every night after everyone had left. This concert would be a monumental feather in his cap, as well as hers, and he knew it.

Saturday morning found Meredith sleeping in and drinking tea in her flannel nightgown and cozy warm bathrobe upon rising. After slipping on her Sherpa-lined moccasins, she turned on the heat when she got up, as the cold of fall was starting to slip into the area. There was a light frost on the rooftops, and the chill from the change of the seasons felt good. The doorbell rang at 10:00 a.m. Meredith was surprised, as she wasn't expecting anyone, but went to the door in her bathrobe and peaked around the curtain on the side panel window. The A Arrangement Florist truck was parked out front with the motor on, emitting steamy exhaust out the back in the cold. Meredith opened the door and was handed a huge bouquet of a dozen red roses in a tall vase. She thanked the driver, took them inside, and opened the card. It read, "Knowing that you will be fantastic tonight! Love, Evan." Her heart beamed and skipped a beat. The smell of the roses started filling the room. She stared at the intricate layers of each flower that wound round and round, each flower being formed slightly different from the one next to it. A rose was an amazing creation. This whole relationship was an amazing experience. She picked up her phone and called Evan's number.

"Mr. Sanders," she started after he answered. "Wow. Thank you!"

"I hope they didn't come too early and wake you," he replied. "I told them not to show up before ten."

"No, they came at the perfect time. I was just sitting here enjoying my tea. You really know how to make a girl feel special!"

"That's the plan! Can I pick you up this evening?" Meredith thought for a moment. The concert would begin at eight.

"Well, you could pick me up at six fifteen, having me over there no later than six thirty, and then disappear. I mean really disappear. I need to warm up alone and have some down time to just relax and get composed. I wouldn't see you until after the concert. Would that be okay?"

"That's perfect," Evan said.

"And I really mean I need my alone time," said Meredith. "It's very important to my playing success."

"Yes, ma'am," he replied dutifully.

"No kissy-huggy stuff," she said with a grin.

"Yes Ma'am. Totally understood." She could envision him smiling with those dimples of his punctuating his face. "I will see you at six fifteen sharp."

"Thanks, Evan," she said sincerely. "I really appreciate the support and especially the roses."

"Yes, ma'am." With that, he said his goodbyes and hung up.

What a prize he is, she thought as she went back to her tea. How she lucked into finding someone like Evan she wasn't quite sure, but she cherished the relationship they were slowly building between them. She would miss him today during her alone time. She would really miss him.

Meredith spent the day loafing and relaxing. At four thirty, she took a hot steamy bath, washed her hair, and piled it on top of her head. She began applying makeup, going lightly on the foundation but making her large eyes pop with discreetly applied liner and brown shadow. She preferred to do her own hair and makeup so she looked like herself instead of like some clown.

At quarter to six, she took out her long rust-colored strappy gown of soft crepe that fitted her slim waist, fanning out slightly from her hips to the floor at the bottom. She stepped into matching pumps. The striking fall color was bright and rich enough that she would stand out in front of the black of the piano and the outfits of orchestra members, making her the focal point of attention. The only jewelry she wore was the silver pair of drop earrings given to her by her parents. She sat at the piano, ran some scales, and ran the beginning of the three movements of the Rachmaninoff.

The doorbell rang precisely at six fifteen, and Evan entered, looking dashingly handsome in his black tuxedo. Meredith's heart skipped a beat when she saw him all dressed up for the first time. His two dimples stood out as he gave her that smile that played on her heartstrings. He stopped and just stared at her, not believing how beautiful she was.

"I don't know what to say," he said. "You look incredibly lovely. I admit I feel kind of tongue-tied, like I'm staring at a princess." He just stood there and gazed at her. She could feel his admiration radiating across the room. It felt good to feel the attention of a man. It had been so long, if ever, that she had felt what she was feeling now.

Meredith smiled. "We'd better go." She locked up, and they left the house after he opened the car door for her. They rode to the green room at Twitchell, where Meredith would be warming up. It was a soundproof room below the stage and the venue itself, and she could play as loud as she liked and not be heard.

When they arrived, she said, "Now remember," you promised to leave.

"I remember." He smiled. "And don't forget to break a leg!" He kissed his index finger and blew the kiss her way as he left, closing the door behind him. She did all she could to relax and push him out of her mind as she readied herself for the concert. She always needed time alone before a performance. She did a few warm-ups but basically prepared her inner self for the experience of sharing her music with the audience. She pulled up past memories of confidence she experienced at past concerts and imagined herself walking on this stage, on this night, and feeling those same feelings. She was a strong woman despite her delicate appearance. Sitting down at the piano, her fingers ran through the warm-ups, but her mind was elsewhere, mustering up all the feelings of confidence, poise, and control that had always led her through her music. Her music was inside her. Tonight she would share it with the audience. The anticipation of the whole experience was always as exciting as the performance.

Twitchell was noisy as people came in chatting, removing their coats, and taking their seats. It was always slightly noisy before concerts, a kind of excited noisiness that anticipated the thrill of the music that was to come. The seats were filling up fast. The hall itself had been restored to the glory of its original beauty of earlier days and was a fitting background for the performance to come. It was an acoustical wonder.

The orchestra members wandered onto the stage one by one, taking seats and warming up individually. The lights were still on, and the noise level increased as the clock ticked away the minutes before the performance would begin. Slowly the lights dimmed, and a silent hush fell over the audience. Applause filled the room as the concert mistress entered, acknowledged her applause, and faced the orchestra. She nodded to the first chair oboe to play an "A," and then she tuned the various sections of the orchestra and sat down.

Then strong applause rang out as Meredith entered followed by Dr. Prentice. She glowed from within and shared her inner being with her audience through her wide eyes and radiant smile. She entered with shoulders back and head held high, displaying an air of confidence that was picked up immediately by the audience. They could tell by her poise and demeanor that they were in for a musical treat. Evan sat there watching her so proudly, feeling honored that he had been allowed to be a part of her life.

9

The key to the mystery of a great artist, is that for reasons
unknown, he will give away his energies and his life to
make sure that one note follows the other, and leaves us
with the feeling that something is right with the world.
　　　　　　　　　　　　　　　　　—Leonard Bernstein

Meredith sat down at the large Steinway placed center stage and
adjusted her bench, her dress, and her frame of mind. Dr. Preston
raised his baton and waited. Meredith would begin the concerto herself, playing solo at the start.

As she began, it was amazing to some in the audience that such
strength, such power, and such authority could come from someone
of her tiny stature. She immediately took command of the performance, and the tone she set caught on like a wildfire amidst the rest
of the orchestra. They were one, and the audience became one with
them, becoming entranced by the beauty of what they were experiencing. Little old ladies who were usually digging in their purses rattling candy wrappers trying to sooth tickling throats were perfectly
silent. Fidgety husbands who had accompanied their music-loving
wives sat still. People with normally wandering eyes who came to be
seen rather than to listen were frozen as the haunting melodies sang
through the hall, all under the leadership of Meredith's playing. The
mood of sweet sadness surrounded all present and brought the listeners to a place of heightened pleasure.

At the end of the first movement, no one moved. Eyes, ears,
and bodies were frozen, waiting and wanting more of what they had
just heard. After a brief pause, Meredith began the soft, sweet melody of the second movement, holding the same magnetic control

of her audience. The liveliness of movement three was followed by the somberness and softness of the closing chords. Meredith and the orchestra froze as the last chord sounded and the audience sat silently still in solemn unity with them. Not a soul moved until Meredith lifted her hands from the piano keyboard. Then came the thunderous applause with shouts of "Bravo" ringing through the hall as the applause got louder and louder like an approaching train. Meredith stood, took a long bow, and left the stage followed by a beaming Dr. Preston. The cheering and yelling got stronger and more intense as Meredith entered alone this time to continue her bows center stage. People began standing, and soon the entire audience was standing as shouts of "Encore" and "Bravo" could be heard through the intense clapping that would not stop. Meredith always had an encore ready. She always played something uncomplicated and familiar that most listeners could recognize and identify with. She sat down at the piano to make the audience stop yelling and clapping. She faced the audience and stated, "Debussy's 'Clair de Lune.'" She received a few *ah*'s from the audience, but then everyone respectfully became quiet. Soon the flowing, sweet melody of the piece sang through the hall as people listened and enjoyed the peacefulness of the music. Upon finishing, Meredith took a long bow and then walked off. The applause began again and would not stop. Shouts of "More" and "Another" were yelled above the thunder. Finally, Meredith came out and sat at the piano once more.

Immediate silence returned. She announced, "Brahms 'Intermezzo Opus 117 No. 2,'" followed by a few cheers, and then silence. Following the end of the piece, the president of the Music Foundation came out and presented her with a bouquet of roses. Dr. Preston entered, took her hand, and they both bowed together, followed by his acknowledgment of the orchestra, the concert mistress, and the individual sections. He then acknowledged Meredith again, as the unbroken clapping continued. Pure joy filled her soul, as she knew she had done her very best. This was what it was all about—the pure and simple unity with the orchestra, the beauty of the music, the sharing of who she was from deep within herself, a union she could never create in any other manner. It was what she had spent her life working to achieve. It was everything that mattered to her.

Evan stood smiling at his chair with the symphony, pleased that he could watch her enjoy the results of her years and years of practice and devotion to her craft. He looked at the woman he was beginning to love, wondering if he could ever mean as much to her as her enjoyment of her music and her performing obviously meant to her. He had shared one brief day with her. She had shared a lifetime with her music. He watched her leave the stage for the last time, knowing what a precious jewel of a woman she was, trying not to imagine that he might have to compete with her music for a prime spot in her heart. If that were the case, he felt surely he would be the loser.

The crowds surrounded Meredith in the outer lobby. Little old ladies who attended all of the concerts bashfully came up for her autograph as well as some of the financial backers of the arts in Spartanburg and those attending their first concert in town. They all surrounded Meredith, wanting to meet the woman who had captivated them with her playing. She patiently shook hands and spoke to each one, satisfying their desire to feel more a part of the concert experience.

As the last hand-shaker left, she turned to find Evan standing there, beaming with pride and joy at the amazing woman he had been privileged to come to know in the last few weeks. He gently kissed her cheek and took a step backward, admiring her beauty, her poise, and the glow she radiated from her accomplishment.

"What can I say!" he declared. "You were magic, sheer magic!" He just stood there, smiling and watching her with pride! She shyly smiled back. One of the qualities he loved about her was her complete humility. She totally did not see the aura of her fame nor did she have the quality of feeling better than everyone else. On the contrary, she would pull the good qualities out of everyone else to the surface, overlooking her own and minimizing her importance.

"Dr. Preston is having a small reception at his house for the Music Foundation, and you are invited to come too," she announced. "I told him if they wanted me, they had to invite you too! I said you were a captive prisoner!" She loved toying with him. "Seriously, I was told to bring a guest."

"Well, in that case, I am honored to be your guest," he said as he bowed from the waist in royal fashion. "I will feel like the prince accompanying Cinderella to the ball."

"Yes, the charming prince," she added, toying with him again but really meaning it at the same time.

"Just don't disappear like Cinderella did," he joked. "I'll never make it back to Asheville if my Jeep turns into a pumpkin."

"I will stay totally within your sight," she promised. "Dr. Preston gave me verbal directions, so hopefully we can find it. He just lives on Otis Boulevard in Converse Heights. I've been told it's a pretty house. I love going to pretty houses."

Lights in the auditorium were being turned out by the technical staff, as Evan and Meredith made their way through the hall to the parking lot. Dr. Preston saw them on their way out from the other side of the hall and smiled at the two of them leaving together, as they did make a handsome couple. He seemed pleased but not totally surprised that they had become a twosome.

Evan pulled onto Otis Boulevard, and they saw the long line of cars parked on both sides of the road in front of the stately two-story brick Georgian home. Sparkling crystal chandeliers shone from the front rooms as they made their way up the stone path to the giant white pillars of the front porch. Mrs. Preston came to the glass-and-wood porch door as they stepped onto the elegant small slate porch. "Welcome! I'm Helen Preston. Meredith, it is an honor to have you come to our home," she said as she extended her hand.

"Thank you very much! This is Evan Sanders," beamed Meredith as he shook hands with Mrs. Preston. "He plays first cello with the orchestra and comes to us from UNC Asheville."

"No wonder the cello section sang out so beautifully." She smiled. "Excuse me for one brief moment. I hear Bill coming in through the back door."

Bill Preston came immediately to the front door and gave Meredith a strong, loving hug. "You completely stunned our audience! They were not expecting the show you gave them. Bravo! "He hugged her again with obvious joy, as Helen and Evan supported his show of approval. Bill held his hand out to Evan.

"Nice job, Evan. We'll have to have you join us again in the future." Evan smiled and hoped that was the case.

"Come into the living room," he said, obviously speaking to Meredith, "and I'll introduce you to our guests. They are anxiously awaiting to meet the girl who set the place on fire!"

The house was an old Georgian beauty restored in glorious fashion. A rich mahogany handrail topped the winding semicarpeted staircase that led to the upstairs. The original hardwood floors throughout the house displayed rich Oriental carpets and runners comprised of intricate patterns of golds, bright maroons, browns, and blacks. The carpets stood out in contrast to the cream-colored walls and heavy, solid white crown molding. Rounded doorways led from room to room and complimented the floor-to-ceiling beveled glass-paned windows. Large crystal chandeliers in the living room and dining room sparkled and lit up the stunning paintings framed in gold. Large mirrors and just the right accessories and lamps finished each room to perfection. A fern here or a green plant there added color and warmth to the room filled with welcoming stuffed chairs and handsome couches. A blazing fire roared in the black marble-faced fireplace, adding warmth and sophistication to the elegance of the room. The home could have been pictured in a *House Beautiful* magazine.

Meredith made the rounds with Dr. Preston, being introduced to many of the wealthy patrons who gave money to support the arts in Spartanburg. Evan took a back seat to Meredith and made his way to the dining room. The table was filled with a wonderful array of scrumptious hors d'oeuvres. Observing the display and taking a plate of some kind of expensive china, he began piling the finger foods on his plate. Fresh shrimp with sauce, stuffed mushrooms, miniature broccoli quiches, baby egg rolls, crackers with artichoke dip, and small breaded pieces of chicken, were only a few of the nibbles he selected. The other side of the table held the sweet selections, including fancy cookies, lemon squares, baklava, iced chocolate brownies, gingerbread squares, and Godiva chocolates. Upon filling his plate, he was given a glass of champagne in a crystal flute by a waiter dressed fashionably in a black tailcoat.

Evan introduced himself to a few of the guests who came in to partake of the refreshments and found out that he had more in common with these people than he would have originally thought. They were just people like himself, most of them older but sporting interesting lives. They were welcoming people, who seemed genuinely interested in him and could have been family. He didn't really know what the experience of family felt like since his parents had really kept him at arm's length and had not become involved in who he was and what he did. He felt at home here. It felt very festive. He was having a good time when Meredith came in to take a plate and partake of the goodies. She apologized for leaving him alone for so long, but after he told her what a good time he was having, she was pleased. Dr. Preston was beaming with pride at how the whole evening had come out. Everything, from the opening note to the drinking of the final cup of coffee, had been a success.

Helen Preston came and chatted a bit with Meredith. She confided that she had raised two grown boys but that she would have loved to have had a daughter like Meredith. Meredith was touched by her comment. Helen seemed sweet, sincere, and genuinely interested in Meredith and her career. They ended their chat with Helen saying she would love to have Meredith "and her gentleman" come for dinner sometime soon. Meredith felt that she really meant it.

As the guests began leaving, Dr. Preston hugged Meredith again, telling her how very proud he was of her. Helen Preston again thanked them both for coming, and Meredith and Evan made their way out the door to Evan's car.

Evan slowly pulled up in front of Meredith's house on Palmetto Street and turned off the ignition.

"What an evening," Meredith commented as she looked at Evan with merriment in her eyes. "I don't think things could have gone any better than they did."

"I agree," Evan commented.

"Would you like to come in for a glass of wine by the fire?" Meredith asked. "Or maybe some tea since you have a long drive ahead of you. I know I'm stuffed, but something to drink would be kind of nice."

"Wine would be perfect," Evan said. "And the fire would be wonderful." She got tickled as he made his regular trek around the front of the Jeep to open her door. It was one of the many sweet things she loved about him. The chill in the evening air definitely announced that fall had arrived in the upstate. Evan put his arm around Meredith's bare shoulder and rubbed it briskly to erase the goose bumps. They hurried up the steps, anxious to get inside, out of the cold fall air.

"Your house is really charming," Evan commented. "Can I build a fire while you get the wine?" Meredith chuckled.

"That would be lovely, except all you have to do is press a button. I have gas logs!"

"A cheater," replied Evan! "Aha! No *House Beautiful* awards for you!"

"Well, the logs came with the house," said Meredith, "and I must admit that when I come home tired from a long day at school, it's awfully nice just to turn them on and collapse on the couch."

"Okay," mused Evan, "I'll go *mash* the button!" They both laughed.

"Did you notice that the Prestons' fireplace was the real thing?" added Evan.

"I did, and it added such warmth and charm to the already beautiful room," Meredith commented.

"As did you," Evan said. He gazed sweetly at her as he said this.

"I'll get the wine," she said, avoiding the compliment and heading to the kitchen. He followed her.

"We have a lot to choose from," she said.

"Ah, a connoisseur," he remarked.

"I particularly love the red wines, so I don't usually purchase a lot of white, unless it's a Riesling. I have Merlot, Cabernet, Pinot noir, and Malbec."

"What do you recommend?" Evan asked.

"Malbec is my favorite." Meredith smiled. "It is strong, with character," she added.

"Just like you." He was playing this for all it was worth. "Let's have two Malbecs," he ordered.

"Coming right up!"

Evan surveyed the kitchen as Meredith got out the large wine glasses specifically for reds. The knotty pine cabinets and heart-of-pine floors were the originals, updated by the granite countertops, new knobs, and stainless-steel appliances. A brick wall on the back of the kitchen opened on to a screened porch facing an array of giant oak trees, which were about to lose their leaves in the late fall. A country French table sat in front of a side window, facing the neighboring house, which was hidden by huge hardwoods. In the center of the room stood a nice large island.

Meredith carefully opened the corked bottle of wine, pouring a glass for each of them. She carried the wine to the living room, being careful not to spill the precious red liquid. She set the glasses on the coffee table in front of the fireplace, and they both sat down on the couch.

"Mmmm…perfect," said Evan as he sampled the wine. "Strong, with character!"

"Yes." She smiled.

"Well, how does it feel now that it's all over?" Evan asked.

"I don't know. I'm still riding on the high of the concert. That usually lasts for a little while, and then I feel a little down when I realize that it's finished. But there's always more to come in the future, and that keeps me slightly excited all of the time. My students are wonderful. Motivating them and watching them change is exciting, and I wouldn't like the performing as much without the teaching. They balance each other out nicely."

She looked at Evan a bit sadly when she said this. "What about you? Are you finished teaching here now, or will you be coming back?"

Evan stared at her for a moment. He was looking at the big brown eyes and the sweet expression on her face. She was looking back at the dimples, the swig of hair that always hung on his forehead, and the blue of his eyes. She waited for his answer with silent anticipation.

"I'll be coming back for certain," Evan said. Then he paused, not knowing how to go on. But he did. "There's a certain young lady here whom I can't seem to get out of my mind, who somehow is occupying my every thought. I don't think I could stand to be away from her for very long." He looked sweetly at her. There. He had said it. It was out in the open now. Meredith blushed as she looked down for a moment. Then looking up, her eyes met his. He leaned forward and softly kissed her on the mouth with an incredible gentleness. Meredith felt that warm, exciting feeling rush up through her body again. Holding the angelic face that he adored in his hands, he kissed her again, not being able to get enough of her. Meredith gave in to her feelings and kissed him back with all the love and all the feeling that had been welling up inside her for so long.

When they stopped for air, Meredith smiled and said, "I feel like we're two teenagers making out on the sofa after a hot date!"

Evan smiled. "Meredith, my Meredith. Where are we on all of this? We're not two teenagers. We're two adults who are grown and have established lives of our own in different cities. Somehow we've each come this far without becoming attached to anyone, and now, this all seems too good to be happening."

Meredith smiled back and said as sincerely as she could, "Evan, I've never felt like this before. Honestly. But I need time to trust my feelings. This has all happened so fast. But it seems so right. So very right." Putting his arms around her, he stopped her speech with another long kiss, wanting more than he knew he had any right to have. He looked in her eyes again.

"Good," he confided. "That's what I wanted to hear. That makes everything perfect. Complicated but perfect!"

He stared with love into her luminous brown eyes, loving the honesty and sensitivity he saw there. Then he stopped and paused, almost as if he were deciding what to do. "I'm going to go now. I know you'll want to sleep in tomorrow, so I'll call in the early afternoon. You need your rest after a night like this!"

"Please finish your wine," she insisted.

"Yes, so I can be strong with character," he added. Evan finished the last few drops out of his glass, staring at Meredith as he did so.

"This will make me sing all the way to Asheville," he joked as he emptied the last drop of wine from his glass. He put down the glass, stood, and went to the door, with Meredith following.

"Thank you," said Evan sincerely. "Thank you for coming into my life!" And he truly meant what he said. He kissed her softly again and left, closing the door behind him. Meredith was overwhelmed with the whole evening. She turned out the lights and headed for her room. How could she sleep after an evening like this. How could anyone sleep after an evening like this! But excitement and all, she conked out when her head hit the pillow.

The phone rang at 1:00 p.m. the next day. The voice on the other end made her smile. "Hey, sleepyhead! Did you get some rest last night?"

"I did, thank you, sir!"

"You'll never guess what's happening up here," he said. "It's snowing! It's really snowing! It's snowing with huge giant white flakes coming down all over the place!"

"Oh my goodness," Meredith exclaimed in disbelief. "It's just gray and foggy and yucky here."

"That difference in temperature of ten or fifteen degrees makes all the difference in the world," Evan said. "We get the white stuff while you get the rain. We'll probably only get a dusting, but it sure is beautiful." Evan sat quietly for a moment and then continued, trying to phrase everything correctly. "I want you to know that I meant everything I said last night. And I know that you did too."

They both just sat quietly for a few moments. "And know that I'd be down there this evening to take you out to dinner in a flash if the roads had cooperated!"

"I know," she said. "I'd have loved to have dinner with you. But don't you dare try to get down here!"

"The Saluda Grade can turn into a skating rink in bad weather. The drivers turn vicious, gritting their teeth, sliding all over the place and trying to beat every other car down the hill. It becomes a real circus out there. Everything folds up when it snows here. They just don't have any real snow removal equipment, turning the whole situation into a nightmare. And sometimes the white stuff hangs around on the roads for days. But this should melt relatively quickly, being that it's the first snow."

"Well, I'm just going to stay here, drink my tea and hope that you will stay put as well," said Meredith. "You have to promise me, all right?"

"I will," Evan promised. And then he added, "But I'll be thinking of you."

10

To stop the flow of music would be like the stopping of time…
incredible and inconceivable.
—Aaron Copland

T hings were back to normal at Converse on Monday morning. The snow never touched Spartanburg as expected. Meredith was teaching her 9:00 a.m. lesson when a knock came at the door. A student she didn't know came in.

"Dr. Preston wants you to come to his office as soon as your lesson is finished. He said to reschedule your nine thirty lesson and come as soon as you can." If Meredith had family in the area, she would have thought that someone had died, but since she didn't, she was a little less upset than if she had.

The lesson was about finished, so after speaking with her student, she taped a quick note on her door to her nine thirty student and walked down the hall rather quickly to Dr. Preston's office.

"Come in," he said, "and close the door." Bill Preston looked excited, but Meredith had no idea on earth what this could be about. "You had a call from your agent in New York, and I insisted on taking it so as not to disturb your lesson. After reluctantly fighting with me that he had to speak to you personally, he went on and asked for our permission to release you."

"Release me," said Meredith, puzzled as ever.

"Yes," Bill Preston replied. "I gave it to him."

"What is this all about?" demanded Meredith.

"The Czech National Symphony Orchestra in the Czech Republic is doing the Rachmaninoff this weekend. Their star soloist has broken her arm. They need someone to replace her. Your agent has secured the position for you, if you want to accept it," he said with a held-back smile.

"If I want to accept it? Goodness, I'd be foolish not to. This could be the break of a lifetime!" Meredith was now overflowing with excitement, and Bill Preston broke out with the smile he had previously been trying to cover up.

"I knew you'd be thrilled," he exclaimed! "You'll have to leave tomorrow morning so you'll have time to get over your jet lag. Practices with the symphony will begin on Wednesday evening. You should be able to fit right in with their orchestra, except for getting used to the new conductor and the language factor, but they'll probably have an interpreter for you if you need one."

"Prague," she exclaimed with delight! "I have never been across the ocean. I have always dreamed of going to Europe. This is just incredible!"

"You'll fly through Rome. They couldn't get a direct flight from Atlanta to Prague because of the short notice, but you'll be spending all of your time in Prague. It will be a quick trip but a wonderful one I'm sure," said Bill. "You'll need to return the following Sunday and will fly from Prague directly to Atlanta. And of course, everything will be paid for. And you will be paid handsomely for filling in on such short notice. Call your agent back and have him make all of the arrangements. That is, unless you don't want to take the concert!" He was half smiling as he said this.

"You've got to be kidding," said Meredith.

"I am," Dr. Preston smiled. "We'll have a world-famous instructor on our piano faculty! I can see it now. New students will be coming here from all over the place, fighting like flies to study with you!" Meredith just blushed, brimming with excitement about going to Europe and actually playing there.

"Now go, famous woman," Dr. Preston teased. "Call your agent back, and come later in the morning to fill me in on any more details."

Meredith almost skipped down the hall. It was near ten, and she had another student coming shortly. She was dying to call Evan and share the news, but she knew that he would be in class too, so she decided she had to wait until lunchtime. She called her agent, who filled her in on more of the details. Her morning passed slowly, and she had to force herself to pay attention to the lessons instead of dreaming about what was to come. It was frustrating not being able to share this with Evan yet, and she couldn't wait to get on the phone instead of half listening to scales and preludes. This was just too incredible to be true.

As Meredith was locking up her studio for the day at 4:00 p.m., she saw a well-dressed young woman in black heels and a dress coat hurriedly walking down the hall as if she were looking for someone. She was slim with flowing long blond hair and a pretty figure.

"May I help you?" asked Meredith as they approached each other, wondering who this woman was. She seemed a little too old to be one of the students. And too dressed up as well.

"I'm looking for Evan Sanders," she stated with an uncertain look upon her face.

"Mr. Sanders only works here part-time," Meredith stated. "He really doesn't have an office."

The woman looked a bit suspicious. She gave Meredith the once-over with her eyes, not knowing whether to believe her or not.

"What, no office? I'm surprised! Can you tell me how I can contact him?"

Meredith's mouth nearly fell open in shock as she heard the woman speak. Not really wanting her to find him, Meredith went on. "He works mostly at UNC Asheville. You'll have to contact him there."

The woman again gave Meredith a look with her eyes, as if trying to size her up with a gaze. "Do you have a number where I can reach him?"

"No," lied Meredith. "I don't."

"Well, would you give him a message for me?" She went on without waiting for a reply. "Tell him Suzanne was here and that she wants to talk to him! And tell him soon." Again she gave Meredith a suspicious glance and walked off without waiting for a reply, clacking her stiletto heels on the tile floors as she went.

How could there be another woman in the life of this precious man she had kissed and just started getting to know? Her heart didn't have room for anymore heartbreak.

When Meredith got home, she dialed Evan, wanting to spill her exciting news but instead filled with questions of jealousy, wondering who this woman was and why she wanted to see him. He picked up immediately.

"Hi." She stopped there, not knowing what to say. She was mad as hell but didn't want to misinterpret anything. There was so much to tell yet so much angry emotion standing in the way.

"Hi yourself. What's up?"

Rather than beating around the bush, she just said it. "Suzanne was here."

"Suzanne," he stammered.

"Yes, Suzanne. She wanted to know where you were." Silence came from the other end of the phone. Neither of them said anything for a few minutes, then Meredith began with the news that all of a sudden didn't seem so exciting anymore. "I'm flying to Prague tomorrow. The Czech National Symphony needs a soloist for the Rachmaninoff on Saturday, and they've offered me the spot."

"You're kidding. That's incredible! When and where do you fly out from?" Evan asked. Meredith spit out the details abruptly, more concerned about Suzanne than her exciting news.

"I leave tomorrow morning, and I'm pretty sure I'll fly out of GSP, but I'm not certain," she said.

"I want to drive you to the airport," Evan blurted out.

"How can you do that? You have class."

"I'll take care of that. I don't know. I want to see you before you go. Call me as soon as you know everything, okay? Promise?"

She sat quietly for a moment, only able to think about this woman named Suzanne and not wanting to believe that Evan had a past with someone he hadn't told her about.

"Okay."

"Meredith," he stuttered. "It's not what you think. I will tell you all about Suzanne."

"Okay," was all she was able to blurt out. She hung up and called Dr. Preston.

"You're just the person I need to speak to," he said. "Your agent called back here since you didn't pick up in your studio. You have a ticket on Delta for tomorrow morning, so you'll need to be at the airport for a 9:30 a.m. flight flying to Atlanta. You layover for several hours in Atlanta and fly Air Italia to Rome, then after a short layover, they fly you direct to Prague, where they'll have a car for you at the airport to take you to your hotel. You'll be staying in an executive suite at the Presidential hotel in Prague on the River Vltava. My guess is that after treatment like that, you won't want to come back to little old Spartanburg," he said, half teasing but half meaning it. Despite what had just happened with Evan, Meredith was half on cloud nine, taking all of this in but still not really believing it could possibly be true.

"What did I miss?" Dr. Preston asked. "Call your agent. Rehearsals are in the evening. Daytimes are free to do as you please. Your contact person is Ms. Maria Braviak, assistant to the director of the symphony. We'll take care of notifying your students for the rest of the week for you. They'll get a nice little break until you return. What else can I say? I'm just so very, very proud of you, Meredith!" He would have given her a hug if she were there.

"I'm still kind of speechless," Meredith replied. "I'll get back to you if I can think of any more questions." The incident with Evan still smoldered inside her.

She thought of Prague and playing there and going to Europe. Europe! Of all the places to be going! In-between the delightful thoughts of Prague came a feeling of disappointment in Evan since he had not previously volunteered to share any information with her about this woman named Suzanne. He had kissed her. He had kissed her with feeling, or so she thought, and she had shared parts of her soul with him that she had never shared with anyone else. She had never had feelings for anyone else like she had for him, and she thought he felt the same way about her. Could she trust him, or was he not the man she thought he was? How could this be happening with him on what should have been one of the most happiest, exciting days of her career.

She ran out and hit the drugstore to pick up a few items she might need for the trip. She was imagining trying to shop in Prague, not knowing the language, and became more excited thinking about the adventure she was about to begin. Her dress had not been cleaned from last week, but she figured it would be fine. She ran to the bank for some cash to take on the trip and figured she'd just have to exchange it for foreign currency when she got there. Luckily she had a passport, which her agent had made her get when she began working with him. Thank goodness he had had the forethought to make her do that.

After running around madly in the house trying to get ready, she threw in a load of laundry so at least she'd have clean underwear for the trip. Her body was racing frantically, and her mind was doing the same thing inside her head. Making herself calm down and slow-down was a difficult task at the moment. Before a concert, she was the epitome of calmness. Now she was a nervous wreck! She made herself sit down in a chair and settle down for a moment.

Then there was a knock at the door. She went to the door, opened it, and saw Evan standing there looking worried and a bit nervous.

"May I come in?"

"Yes, of course." She closed the door, closing out the cold of the nippy fall day but not knowing whether that coldness would be entering this relationship she had so cherished.

"I wish I could come with you," he said. "I worry about you going all that way by yourself. I really do."

"I'll be fine," she said, trying to sound convincing. "I'll have all kinds of people around me for support. They even have an escort for me, meeting me at the airport."

"That's not what I came here to talk about. I came to tell you about Suzanne."

"And just what do I need to know about Suzanne?" she said with a chill in her voice that Evan had never heard coming from this woman whom he felt he was falling in love with.

He knew that wasn't the Meredith he knew speaking, but he understood her hurt. He just stared at her for a moment. He didn't know how to begin. He didn't want to mess this up, but he knew he had to make things right again.

"Meredith, can we sit down?"

"Yes, of course."

He sat down and stared at the big brown eyes and the lovely long brown hair that framed her angelic face. "Meredith, Suzanne was someone who had an affair with my father."

"What," she stammered.

"I didn't want to go into it during our talk in Asheville because it was something I was embarrassed about that took away any possible good feelings I had toward my father. It was one of my hurts, like the hurt you have that you could not share with me. I'm sorry I didn't think I could share it with you then, but I just couldn't at the time."

"No, I thoroughly understand. Go on."

"Suzanne was the reason my father left the area and moved to California with my mother. My mother didn't know about the affair. Suzanne was blackmailing my father and was paid a large sum of money so she wouldn't tell my mother. My father left his business and everything because my mother would have been devastated if she had found out. We thought it was over. She must be wanting more money."

"Oh Evan, I'm so sorry. I didn't know. More than that, I'm so ashamed. Of me. Of what I almost did. Of doubting you. I had no right."

He took her hands in his and began rubbing them gently with his thumbs. He starred into the large brown eyes he had come to adore, saying nothing. She stared into his, seeing the Evan she knew, the Evan she was starting to love.

"Can you forgive me?" Meredith blurted out.

"The question is, can you forgive me?" Evan said. He put his hands on her shoulders, pulling her close to him, and kissed her gently.

She put her head on his shoulder, and he began stroking her long brown hair as tears began flowing down her cheeks. He took out a handkerchief from his pocket and began softly drying her face. They sat for a long while, just embracing each other with loving kindness.

Finally, Evan chimed in, "Will you just stay away from all of those good-looking European men who will be making eyes at you!

You are far too pretty and far too attractive for them to ignore you! Will you come back to me, my Meredith?"

"How could I not," she replied. With that, he kissed her again, still stroking her long silky hair.

"What time do you want me to pick you up?" Evan said.

"I have to be there for a 9:30 a.m. flight. It's late already. I can offer you my couch and a soft pillow."

"That would be lovely," he said.

"Evan," she blurted out, "know that I can't go any further than that right now. That's just who I am. I have to be who I am."

"And I respect that," he said. "I love who you are." And with that comment, he kissed her again. "Now go get me that soft pillow and maybe a blanket too."

"Okay," she replied, quickly appearing with a pillow and a blanket.

"What are you doing about your classes you have to teach tomorrow?" Meredith asked inquisitively, changing the subject and sounding distinctly like his mother.

"I think I feel a touch of the flu coming on." Evan coughed. "It must be something that's going around down here. I think I'll need a day to get over it."

"Oh, I get it," she remarked. "Just don't pass it on to me when you are here, mister."

"Yes, ma'am," he replied.

"I really need to pack now and then get to bed."

"I think if I put my head on the pillow, I will conk out," he said. "Can we leave the fire on? It will put me to sleep."

"Sure." She kissed him gently on the cheek and went into the bedroom, closing the door behind her. She was relieved. She was in love. She was going to Prague!

When she had jammed everything she thought she could possibly need into her suitcase, she jumped into bed and did actually fall asleep from sheer exhaustion!

11

Without music, life would be a mistake.

—Friedrich Nietzsche

They got to the airport the next morning ahead of schedule. When the bags were checked and on their way down the conveyor belt, Evan told Meredith he had something he wanted her to take with her on the trip, so they sat down for a moment on one of the benches. He pulled out a St. Christopher's medal that was on a gold chain. He explained that St. Christopher would watch over her if she carried the medal with her on her journey. She was touched that he had thought to bring it for her and thanked him sincerely as he put it around her neck and secured the clasp. She promised she would wear it on her the entire trip to receive St. Christopher's protection and to think of Evan.

"Are you Catholic?" Meredith asked.

"Well, I'm one of those people who started out Catholic, but I don't quite make it to church anymore," he admitted a bit painfully, as if he were speaking to a confessor. "Without trying to be disrespectful, I call people like me A&P Catholics. We show up in church twice a year, once for ashes and once for palms!"

"That's terrible." Meredith giggled. "Actually I guess I could put myself in that category as well. I used to go to the Catholic Church regularly when my parents were alive but then never went again after they passed away."

"But I'm sure St. Christopher will take care of people like us too," Evan said, "so keep the medal with you, especially to repel all of those good-looking European men who will try to hit on you. There's no way they won't notice someone as beautiful as you!"

"I will keep it with me," Meredith said forcefully, slightly raising her voice, wanting him to know she was perfectly capable of taking care of herself. "And, Evan, it will keep you with me too," she said sweetly. "I think it's time for me to go." As they stood up, he kissed her gently but tenderly. "Bye," she said, not really wanting to leave him.

"Bye," he echoed. He stood for a long time watching her go down through the lobby and up the escalator to security. Then she was gone. He was not a person who prayed a lot, but he would pray for her while she was away. There would be an empty place in his heart while she was gone that only she could fill.

The flight to Atlanta was uneventful. The Atlanta airport was crowded as usual. As she approached the Air Italia waiting area, Meredith could hear people chatting in Italian. She had no idea what they were saying, but it was exciting just listening to them.

Soon they all boarded a wide-bodied jet with rows of two seats down each side and a long row of seats down the middle. Meredith felt lucky to get a window seat so she could look out and see where they were. She had never flown across the ocean before. Flying over the water was no more dangerous than flying over land, but somehow it just seemed like it was. After takeoff, her palms felt sweaty as the plane made its usual up-and-down bounces from the air currents. It wasn't flying she was worried about; it was crashing! Yes, crashing was the obvious worry here. She tried unsuccessfully to get thoughts like that out of her head, but she supposed they would be there until the plane touched the ground again in Rome. She watched her little digital map at the back of the seat in front of her that pinpointed exactly where the plane was. Having a window seat, she was privileged to be able to look out and see the exact moment the plane left the land. It was dark outside, but all of a sudden, the tiny lights of the cities and towns she had been watching disappeared into a dark, black nothingness. Dark, cold, and black. She didn't want to think about it.

The person sitting next to her seemed self-absorbed and impersonal and seemed to have the personality of a snail. That was actually a kind way of describing him. He had thinning gray hair, beady little eyes looking through black-rimmed glasses, and a long pointy nose that twitched nervously when she spoke to him. She tried making conversation, but the thought of actually passing the time by talking seemed to freak him out, making him bury his nose in his *New York Times*, as if taking cover. Little did she know that that would be the last she would hear from him for the rest of the trip. Eleven hours in one seat would be a long time, especially sitting next to someone who refused to pass the time of day. Yes, it would be a very long time.

Dinner was really good. No peanuts here. And there was a choice. She chose the steak with complimentary wine. And tiramisu for dessert. Not bad. Not bad at all. Takeoff and dinner had monopolized all of an hour and a half. Now there were only nine and a half more hours to go. Couldn't someone get everyone up and lead a round of group calisthenics or something or maybe a round of charades? Or they could all sing a verse of "She'll Be Comin' Round the Mountain." That would help. Anything so they wouldn't have to just sit there. And now they were turning out the lights. Forced sleeping. They were trying to get everyone to go to sleep sitting up in a chair. Were they nuts? Who could sleep in a chair. And now the handsome steward was coming around with pillows, tiny little squares of pillows with barely any stuffing inside of them. Her doll once slept on a pillow like that. No wonder her doll always slept with her eyes open. She took one to try to convince herself that her chair/bed was a little more comfortable than it was. The agonizing choice was trying to decide whether to put it behind her back or behind her head since everyone got only one pillow.

She had brought a book, but somehow she couldn't think of reading while trying to manage the excitement of the trip. The man beside her was still reading. He'd probably still be reading when they landed in Rome. Rome! She couldn't believe she was going to Rome! She would land in Rome at 10:00 a.m., Italian time. Gracious! That would be 4:00 a.m. South Carolina time, with the six-hour time difference, and she probably would land without having slept a wink. There would be no escort in Rome. She'd have to manage changing gates by herself. Once she landed in Prague and met her escort, she'd let him or her carry her out if need be. Exhaustion would probably trump the excitement of being there, and the only thing of importance would be finding her hotel room, with or without assistance.

Surprisingly enough, Meredith did manage to sleep a bit. When she woke, she opened her window. The bleak darkness of the night had been replaced by the new birth of the beginning day. Radiant golden streaks of light began stealing their way over the eastern horizon of pink-and-orange slivers of sky. A blanket of cottony white clouds hovered below, peaceful and silent. The beauty of the sunrise filled her with awe. People were still sleeping, and the cabin lights were not yet turned on. She reached around her neck, touching the gold St. Christopher's medal Evan had given her, rubbing it gently with her thumbs. St. Christopher had guided them safely across the depths of the ocean. She knew little of St. Christopher, only aware that he was the patron saint of travelers. She vaguely remembered a plastic statue of him her parents had on the dashboard of their car. All he had ever been to her was a plastic statue. She was even less aware of what she felt of her religious beliefs. She believed there was a God. She believed he was in control over what went on in the world, and she even prayed to him in times of doubt and pain or when she really, really needed a favor; but other than that, she really didn't think about God very much. Her life was built on her music.

She thought of Evan. How had she managed to meet such a sweet, attractive man who was so kind and gentle. She felt so comfortable with him and felt like she could talk to him about anything. He was so attentive and so much fun to be with. She had always hoped she would find a soulmate at some point in her life. Evan had all the possibilities. He was beginning to become such an important part of her life. Going through their misunderstanding had made it even better. They would be able to talk about problems and come out the other side.

Looking out the window, Meredith saw the clouds below thinning out as the golden rays of sunlight began brightening up the sky. And below the clouds, everything was totally white again. She only saw mountains—snowy mountains, totally frozen snowy mountains! They had reached the other side of the Atlantic Ocean! Looking on the digital map in front of her, it appeared that they were flying over the Swiss Alps. A thrill of excitement raced through her body as she realized where she was, and all the images in her brain from her childhood of what Switzerland must looked like appeared in her mind. She was flying over a place she had only read about and going to a place she had only learned about in her social studies books in school. Stereotypical ideas of what Switzerland must be like flashed through her mind. She thought of mountain goats standing on snowcapped mountains and yodelers, men wearing lederhosen, and chocolate, lots of chocolate. Yes, the place of her stereotypical image really existed. It actually existed. And she was flying over it all. The thrill of it filled her beyond belief!

All the lights in the cabin suddenly came on, and a flurry of activity began in the isles as trays filled with warm croissants, fresh fruit, yogurt, and orange juice were passed out. The smell of coffee filled the air and made Meredith incredibly hungry and anxious to receive her tray. The dreary man beside her woke up but seemed self-absorbed and angry that the lights had come on and woke him up. He looked like he wanted to crawl back under his *New York Times* and go to sleep. He refused a breakfast tray, appearing annoyed and bothered that they had offered him one. How awful to meet life head-on, feeling angry. Meredith couldn't imagine not wanting to eat after the long night flying across the sea. She was anticipating the excitement that was to come!

After flying over frozen mountains for what seemed to be a very long time, the ice below became replaced by green, beautiful green. They were flying over the section of Northern Italy known as Tuscany. As the plane's altitude became lower, Meredith could see occasional farmhouses with orangey-red roofs and tall pencil-like green cedar trees here and there standing on rolling hills. It appeared to be farm country. It was very beautiful farm country. Pictures she had seen of this area flashed through her mind as she watched the idyllic scenery below pass by. The roofs and cedar trees let her know she was definitely not in America. The flight attendant requested that seat backs and tray tables be returned to their upright position. They were making their final approach into Rome's Fiumicino Leonardo Da Vinci International Airport. The airport appeared to be far away from the city. Tears filled her eyes as the plane touched down. She and St. Christopher had just flown across the Atlantic Ocean. They had made it to Rome! She said a silent prayer of thanksgiving for the safe trip. It was the first prayer she had said in a long time!

It took a good while for all of the people on the huge jumbo jet to deplane. After the man in the seat next to her left, Meredith decided she would let others go off ahead of her so she could easily remove her carry-on luggage from the upper bin without feeling rushed. She had several hours until her flight left for Prague, and she was in no hurry to join the stampede of travelers scrambling for the exit. She was one of the last passengers to leave the plane and sincerely thanked the flight attendants for their fine service during the flight.

As she came out of the Jetway and into the airport itself, there was a flurry of activity going on at the gate exit. A handful of women dressed in white robes trimmed in dark blue were scurrying about close to the exit door as if in preparation for something important that was about to happen. A few of the passengers who had deplaned late with Meredith hung back near the gate to see if they could figure out what was going on. There was a rumor that Mother Teresa of Calcutta** had been traveling in the first-class section of the plane and that they were holding her behind to exit the plane after the majority of the passengers had left the area. Security officials wanted to keep her away from the crowds of people for her safety. The women scurrying about were sisters of the Missionaries of Charity, who were dedicated to serving the poorest of the poor. They were dressed in the traditional white habit with dark-blue stripes that was worn by these selfless women throughout the world. Meredith knew of Mother Teresa and the life of service she had willingly given to the sick and dying in many countries but especially in India. Meredith stood with the rest of the passengers who had hung back, and before long, one of the nuns came out of the Jetway, pushing the world-famous nun in a

---

* Mother Mary Teresa Bojaxhiu, honoured in the Catholic Church as Saint Teresa of Calcutta, was an Albanian Indian Roman Catholic nun and missionary. She was born in Skopje, then part of the Kosovo Vilayet of the Ottoman Empire. (https://en.wikipedia.org/wiki/Mother_Teresa)

wheelchair as the other nuns flocked by her side. Tiny in stature and appearing quite old with sun-tanned-looking skin, she was smiling at the crowd in front of her, beckoning those nearby not to be afraid to come closer. She was calling with her hand and her body language in a voiceless, friendly way. Most of the people just stood still, almost afraid to move closer and frozen in awe of this holy, famous woman. But still Mother Teresa kept motioning with her hand, calling anyone who would approach her to come forward. Meredith felt compelled to go closer. It was like the spell of this woman was drawing her in, almost beckoning to her personally to come. Slowly she approached the wheelchair. There she saw a tiny, old, weathered and wrinkled face of a woman with wide eyes and a loving smile that seemed to fill her tiny face with joy and humility. Meredith slowly stepped closer to her chair and felt a radiation of love coming through those wide eyes directed personally at her. She saw and felt something larger and more powerful than the tiny woman herself. What she felt was coming through the woman, not of her. It filled Meredith with joy and made her feel whole. Mother Teresa motioned to Meredith to come closer and put in her hand a small silver medal as she squeezed her hand. She did not speak, but there was no need for words. The message of unconditional love was clearly coming through her eyes as she stared into Meredith's eyes. It was a tremendously powerful moment for Meredith. Her whole body yearned to remain there in her presence, surrounded by this loving, caring feeling, but the nuns quickly pushed the famous woman away. Meredith stood there, not able to move, watching as they pushed Mother Teresa down the corridor. She stood still, keeping her eyes on them until the group of nuns was out of sight. A warm glow remained in her heart, and she looked down at the small silver medal that had just been placed in her hand. Somehow she was changed. She felt different. She felt that she had just encountered something powerful.

Meredith called Evan from the airport with her prepurchased phone card, letting him know that she had landed safely in Rome. She only spoke for a moment since the call was expensive. She spoke nothing of the encounter with Mother Teresa. There were no words to explain what she had just experienced. She still felt the glow of the encounter and held the small silver medal tightly in her hand as she moved through the airport to find the gate she would disembark from.

The flight to Prague was uneventful. She connected easily with her chauffeur in the airport and was taken directly to her hotel suite. Upon finding everything in order, she collapsed in her bed, thoroughly worn out from the jet lag. She slept until the next morning.

12

When I hear music, I fear no danger. I am invulnerable. I see no
foe. I am related to the earliest of times and to the latest of times.
—Henry David Thoreau

After sleeping in much too long, Meredith got out of bed and
opened the heavy drapes covering the large windows in her room
to reveal rays of golden sun lighting up the roofs and steeples of
the city. Her room was a corner room overlooking the Vltava River.
Seagulls flew about, seeming to enjoy the morning air, and even a
group of white swans huddled beneath a nearby bridge. There were
many bridges and rooftops—orangey red tiled rooftops. They would
turn out to be one of her favorite picture-like memories of the city
of Prague. Taking a closer look, she was impressed by the number
of church steeples. The chalky green domes, many onion-shaped,
and the thin bell towers covering all styles of architecture, including Gothic, Romanesque, and Baroque seemed to be everywhere.
The striking beauty of the old-world town filled her heart. It was
breathtaking.

After taking in the incredible view from her windows, she
immediately took out the small silver medal that had been placed
in her hand by Mother Teresa and examined it carefully. It was oval
in shape and had a full raised figure of the Virgin Mary with out-
stretched hands, standing on the earth with her foot crushing the
head of a serpent. The writing surrounding the Virgin was too small
for Meredith to read at the time. On the back of the medal was a large
M surmounted by a bar and cross, with two large hearts beneath the
M. The word *Italy* was printed under the two hearts, and the letter *M*
and hearts were surrounded by twelve stars. Meredith took the medal

and placed it on the chain around her neck that Evan had given her, holding the medal of St. Christopher. She still felt the glow that had encompassed her during the encounter.

Now she would have two people to guide her on her journey. She knew that St. Christopher was in good company and was determined to find out more about the medal, what the inscription said, and what the symbols on the back of the medal meant.

After taking a steamy, hot shower, she fixed her hair and makeup, dressed in gray slacks and a gray long-sleeved cashmere sweater, and went downstairs to a very lovely breakfast buffet in the dining room. The buffet exceeded all her expectations. Fresh fruits galore, a whole bakery of varied pastries, and all kinds of cold meats and sausages were laid out on long tables accented by arrangements of fresh flowers on pedestals. The presentation was artistic and beautifully done, and the food was fit for the appetite of a king. Boiled and scrambled eggs, hot cooked meats, and various kinds of yogurts were laid out as well. The only thing missing, thought Meredith, were the grits. The Czech Republic was not into grits. Meredith's eyes were bigger than her stomach, but she readily ate all she had taken, even though she usually consumed very little for breakfast. She tried to stay away from the pastry table but wound up taking an iced apple strudel that turned out to be mouthwatering. She had the day free and did not have to appear at rehearsal until early evening. It was already Wednesday. Her traveling and her sleeping upon arrival made the days seem to pass quickly since she had left South Carolina. She actually felt quite good after traveling all that way and passing through several time zones.

After eating breakfast, Meredith took her finger and stroked the outline of the Virgin on the silver medal she wore around her neck, thinking about the small, famous woman who had placed it in her hands. She was determined to find out more about the medal and why Mother Teresa seemed so honored to be passing it out. As she got up to leave, she hoped St. Christopher and the Virgin would make friends as they were hanging closely on the same chain. She was determined to wear both of them for the remainder of her trip.

13

Music in the soul can be heard by the universe.

—Lao Tzu

After putting on the light hip-length khaki jacket she had brought with her and receiving directions from the concierge, Meredith exited the hotel and headed in the direction of the old town square, armed with written directions and a map. The chill of early fall was in the air, and the walk would be refreshing. The way to the old town passed present-day upscale shops such as Gucci, Cartier, and Louis Vuitton. Uninterested in the current-day treasures they held, Meredith's mind wandered back to yesterday's events and the meeting of the tiny old woman with the sun-weathered skin and the magical eyes. It was the image of her eyes that played over and over in Meredith's mind— not the eyes themselves but the light that danced from within them. What Meredith saw and felt was something that came through them. It was something almost magical and unimaginably strong that came from a place or a being far away. Purity, unconditional love, peace, joy, and a lack of fear seemed to be radiating forth. It was as if this magical woman knew of or had tasted something that was currently not present in Meredith's life so far. Serenity had welled up within her upon meeting this woman and had left an imprint on her heart. She wanted to find it again. She wanted to go to it and dwell there. She felt she could stay there always if she could find it again. And she knew that whatever it was, it had never been present in her life. Mother Teresa had left, but the aura of her presence had remained with Meredith in spirit.

The asphalt beneath her feet turned to cobblestone, and as she kept walking, Meredith saw that the buildings with modern storefronts she had just passed were being replaced by old buildings, very old buildings. She was coming into the area known as Old Town. More and more people surrounded her as she came upon the Old Town Square, the center of life in Old Town, Prague. As she walked, she heard German, and French, and Italian being spoken by the hundreds of tourists who were, like herself, excited to be there and anxious to immerse themselves in the spirit of the city. Lovers holding hands strolled together next to groups of giggly young girls dressed in too-tight jeans and spiked high heels. Young men smoking cigarettes, boasting straggly long hair and black leather jackets, mingled with the sweatshirt set of middle-aged couples with slightly wrinkled faces and thin graying hair. Society as a whole had been brought together in this one place by an interest in a town that had been inhabited by people of a time long ago—people who were now gone forever from the face of the earth, people who had made history and lived their lives in this very spot. Meredith wondered about these people who had lived and died here, what they had done and what they had been like. They had had their chance to make their statements, to live their lives, then to pass on and be replaced by the people who now walked the cobblestoned streets. Who were these present-day people? What were their statements? Of what importance did their smoking and their laughing and their strolling have in the whole scheme of things? Most of them would live and die without leaving lasting impressions in their wakes. What did it all mean? Why were they all here? Why did it all matter? They were not the usual cross section of middle-class scholarly students she taught at Converse. They seemed to come from immensely diverse backgrounds. The oldness of the city and the diversity of the tourists seemed to give her a new way of looking at things. It raised many questions in her mind about life and its purpose.

Strong rays of bright sunshine filtered through the cracks between the buildings and made the bright colors and orangey red roofs of the Old Town pop out, drawing attention to the beauty of the city. The square was a jewel of one unique building after another. The ornateness and detail present in each building was striking, contrasted starkly by rows and rows of loosely put-together wooden tables sitting on the cobblestones filled with every kind of souvenir or craft imaginable for sale to those who wanted to take home something tangible, something to remind them of this day and this hour they had spent in this historic place. The selling and the strolling and the talking and the laughing went on day after day, year after year, decade after decade, as the tourists passed through the city with regularity.

Meredith came upon the antique astronomical clock, a high point of Prague that dated back to the fifteenth century. Scores of visitors stood before the ancient timepiece mounted on the southern wall of the Old Town city hall, waiting for the moment, on the hour, when the twelve wooden apostles, now standing still, would silently march before the crowd in front of the onlookers who passed by. Catholicism had been one of the main religions of the past made obvious by the presence of the twelve apostles who marched across the face of this ancient clock. A bony skeleton with a laugh-like smirk standing nearby would then strike the hour, reminding every onlooker that his time on earth would come to an end someday. Hundreds of cameras clicked to record the event that happened hour after hour, day after day, year after year with precise regularity. The clock and its figurines gave Meredith an eerie sense of the shortness of life, an eeriness that also seemed to be felt by the hundreds of onlookers standing and waiting next to Meredith for the striking of the hour.

On the Old Town Square was St. Nicholas's Church, which the guidebook said was a must-see, so Meredith headed in that direction. The gleaming white front of the old Baroque church almost seemed to shine in the sunlight. The book said that Czech army units were stationed there during World War II while the church was being restored and that today it was used as a venue for classical concerts. Upon entering, tourists were overwhelmed by the beauty of the dome paintings showing scenes from the lives of St. Nicholas and St. Benedict. Gold leaf laced the pillars and sculptures and statues, making the church seem like a palace fit for a king. Not ever having been to Europe before, this was the first of the many grand European churches that Meredith would see. She was astonished with the beauty of it all. And as she left, she spied a rack of pamphlets written in different languages. Right in front of her was a pamphlet written in English about the miraculous medal she wore given to her by Mother Teresa. She snatched the pamphlet from the rack and placed it in her purse.

Upon leaving the church, she decided to combine her lunch and dinner in one meal since she had eaten breakfast late and would be picked up early for rehearsal by her assigned assistant for the concert. Upon consulting her guidebook, she chose Staromacek Restaurant, just off the Old Town Square, known for its Bohemian cooking. As she entered, a waiter in traditional costume led Meredith to a table dressed in a green linen tablecloth and a small vase of fresh flowers. The room itself felt very old world yet comfortable, warm, and friendly. She chuckled as she read the menu, noticing that they served many different kinds of rabbit dishes. Not caring to dine on Peter himself, she decided on a cup of broth with noodles and beef, followed by roast pork with cabbage and potato dumplings. Finding the dinner itself to be wonderful, she chose a warm apple strudel with fresh whipped cream for dessert. As she rose to leave, she wondered if she would be able to perform that evening with such a full belly!

The walk back to the hotel was interesting as she noticed new details on the very same buildings and streets she had passed going to the square that morning. A bit of gold scrollwork here or a bit of decorative edging there jumped out in a striking way that it had not done on the first trip through the street. Hand-painted frescos revealed people and events unseen on her first walk down the street as she stopped and stared at them. One could stare at them for hours, noticing new minute details with each examination. Finally reaching the hotel feeling somewhat tired, she flopped on the bed and took a short nap in preparation for the evening's rehearsal.

14

Music is the universal language of mankind.
—Henry Wadsworth Longfellow

D ressed in comfortable black slacks and a black tunic, Meredith met Maria Braviak downstairs in the lobby with a sense of heightened excitement. Maria would look after her this week during her stay in Prague. Maria—as she requested Meredith call her—spoke Czech, Slovak, English, Italian, and German. She apparently spoke all of them fluently, which impressed Meredith immensely. She was a slender, intelligent, friendly middle-aged woman whose life was apparently devoted to running the business end of the orchestra. As they got into a waiting car, she explained that they would be going to the Smetana Concert Hall in the Municipal House, which was home to the Czech National Symphony. Besides containing décor from past famous Czech painters and sculptors, the Art Nouveau design and brilliant acoustics of the building were enhanced by a seating capacity for 1,200. It was currently considered one of the most stunningly beautiful buildings in Prague, with its huge glass dome and ornate embellishments. Upon entering the hall itself, Meredith couldn't believe that she was playing in a venue like this. Maria told Meredith that she would leave and that the hall would be hers for an hour and a half before orchestra members started drifting in to be seated and warmed up. Meredith thanked her and said she appreciated the time alone.

Overcome with a sense of awe and a true humbleness of heart, Meredith stepped upon the stage and approached the giant Steinway that had been awaiting her arrival. Looking out into the darkness and still quietness of the hall, she began to develop a deep respect for its history and sheer elegant beauty. She thought of all the performers, famous or otherwise, who had stood here to relish their moment of glory in this very spot. Now it was her turn. It was her turn to dazzle a faceless audience that would come, leave, and then disperse into the society outside that was living and breathing, laughing and loving, and experiencing life in all of its fullness. Her hand touched the two medals that hung around her neck. She traced the outlines of St. Christopher and Mary. She prayed a silent prayer that she would be able to give her best to this experience she was on the threshold of diving into.

The sounds of the grand Steinway warmly melted into the large hall and filled it with melodies that enhanced the beauty of the surrounding art and architecture. The acoustics were incredible. Meredith threw herself, body and soul, into the glorious flow of the Rachmaninoff and became lost in the rapture of the music as it captured her heart and took her to a place of pleasure and ecstasy. She played with a deep passion, not paying attention to time, and was unaware of the tall, slender silhouette of Maria Braviak who quietly stepped upon the stage, vastly impressed by the sounds and emotions that were pouring forth from Meredith and the Steinway. Meredith saw the image of the attractive woman in the corner of her eye and immediately stopped playing when she realized the presence of the stately woman, who was delighted with what she heard and felt while Meredith played. "You have immense talent, my dear! Had you continued, you would have taken me with you to the place where your heart was dwelling! I can see we have selected the proper soloist for this weekend's concert!" Meredith smiled and thanked the woman for the compliments but was untouched, as always, by the magnitude of what had been said.

Meredith left the stage momentarily to freshen up in the restroom and returned to the hall to meet Paul Brennan, the chief conductor and artistic director of the symphony. She had not expected him to be an American and was inwardly delighted that he was, knowing that communication would not be a problem now. He was tall, slender, and distinctively handsome, dressed in nice jeans, a bone turtleneck, and a navy Ralph Lauren blazer, which would come off soon after the rehearsal began. He seemed pleased with Meredith and the overflowing amount of compliments Maria Braviak had made about her playing while she had been freshening up. Apparently Maria Braviak was usually stingy with the compliments she gave out, and her approval of Meredith meant in advance that things should go very well.

The rehearsal did go well. Meredith was delighted playing under the baton of Paul Brennan, who amazingly spoke English. He gave fresh insights to the piece that made it come alive in a new way. He seemed pleased with the way Meredith followed him and his new approach since she had worked with the music for a long time by herself and under different directors. Following the rehearsal and much praise for her playing, he invited her out for a drink. She politely refused, making the excuse that she was still trying to overcome the effects of the jet lag. He smiled with understanding and said maybe they could do it another night. She chuckled inwardly, remembering how Evan had been worried about foreign men making advances.

Upon reaching the hotel, she called Evan on her phone card and reached him on the first try. "Hey stranger," she began. "It's so good to hear your voice."

"Hey!" replied Evan. "I can't believe I'm actually talking to you from the other side of the world. I'm so glad to hear your voice too."

"What time is it there?" Meredith asked, picking up on the sleepiness in his voice.

"Well, it's about 4:00 a.m."

"Oh Evan, I'm so sorry. I wasn't thinking. I'm riding on such a high after our first rehearsal."

"That's okay. It's been downright lonely here! I haven't had anyone to tease!" Meredith relaxed a bit.

"I know. I've been alone, too, a good bit since I got here in spite of being in the midst of millions of people, but it's actually been enjoyable. I've done a good bit of sightseeing, and it's been fun!" She relayed some of the goings-on of the day but couldn't mention Mother Teresa. She had no words that would convey that experience right now. "The rehearsal was amazing. It was so much fun playing under a new conductor. My body is still racing inside. It will be hard to calm down and go to sleep. The conductor is actually an

American, so there is no language barrier. And, Evan, he did try to hit on me. He asked me out for a drink tonight!"

"Well, I hope you told him you were a taken woman," replied Evan. "Maybe you ought to overdo the makeup and clothes tomorrow night and wear some ugly glasses or tease your hair or something."

"I'm a big girl, Evan. I can take care of myself," she replied.

"I know you can! Just know how much you mean to me."

"I do," she said sincerely.

"I have missed you so much," he replied. The phone clicked several clicks and then went dead. The phone card must have run out, so that was the end of the call. She stroked St. Christopher hanging on her necklace and the Virgin hanging next to him as she slowly walked back to her room. Even despite all of the exciting activity, she missed Evan. A lot. The image of his dimpled smile and the memories of his warm touch brought contentment to her heart and happiness to her soul.

As she put on her nightgown, she reviewed the goings-on of the day, feeling like years had passed since she had left Spartanburg. So much had happened in such a short amount of time. The world had become different all of a sudden. She had been thrown into a new time zone, almost without her approval. It was thrilling and exciting but different.

She pulled out the pamphlet that she had taken from the rack in the church in the Old Town and read it with heightened curiosity.

The design of the miraculous medal, as it was called, was given to Saint Catherine Labouré in a vision of the Virgin Mary in Paris in 1830. In the vision, St. Catherine was told to have a medal made according to the directions given by Mary. The article stated that all who wore the medal around the neck with confidence would receive great graces. The hearts on the back of the medal were the hearts of Jesus and Mary, one crowned with thorns and the other pierced with a sword.

The purpose of Mother Teresa giving out medals in the airport became more clear to Meredith. The saintly woman was obviously devoted to the Virgin, evidenced by her life's work of charity to the poor. Yet there was more to it than that. She wanted to draw everyone else in. She wanted everyone to experience the unconditional love that she so confidently radiated from her very being. And Meredith had been given the gift of being a receiver of this experience. It was truly a gift.

Meredith took her fingers and stroked the outline of the Virgin on the silver medal she wore around her neck, remembering the image of the small but powerful woman who had placed it in her hands. She would wear the medal and the medal of St. Christopher Evan had given her for the rest of the trip. What other experiences on this trip were to come that she would treasure?

15

Music can name the unnamable and communicate the unknowable.
—Leonard Bernstein

That night, her dreams toyed with her new experiences. The smiling, loving face of Mother Teresa passed back and forth in front of scenes of the city. Echoes of the Rachmaninoff played over and over as Paul Brennan skipped through the Old Town, leading the tourists who were also skipping through the streets in a straight line, encouraging them with his waiving baton like the Pied Piper. Maria Braviak stood smiling in approval. The images were happy but all mixed up together. They swirled round and round in a glassed in area while the skeleton from the astronomical clock kept chiming away the hours. Evan kept knocking on the glass, trying to get in and join the frenzy; but the more he knocked, the faster the people skipped and danced and laughed and the louder the skeleton chimed, finally waking Meredith up with a jolt. She stared at her clock in the dark and saw that it was only 2:00 a.m. The dream frightened her for a moment, but then she lay down and went back to sleep after some tossing and turning, this time not waking until the alarm went off.

16

So long as the human spirit thrives on this planet, music
in some living form will accompany and sustain it.
—Aaron Copland

Another day had dawned. Meredith was anxious to do more sightseeing. This might be the only time in her life she would get to see
Prague and all of the treasures it held. After hungrily devouring her
breakfast, she took off for the Jewish cemetery, another highlight of
Prague for her to see upon the recommendation of the concierge.

The cemetery dated back to the first half of the fifteenth century, with the oldest tombstone dating back to 1439. Twelve thousand tombstones were present. It was said that when the cemetery
would fill up, new earth would be brought in to add new layers. The
cemetery supposedly contained several burial layers, one on top of the
other, with inscriptions on the tombs written in Hebrew. Men were
required to wear hats before being admitted into the cemetery walls.
Meredith noted that this was very different from the Catholic faith
since in the Catholic faith, it was the women who used to be required
to cover their heads before entering a church. She had childhood
memories of her mother clipping tissues to her head with bobby pins
to fulfill the requirements. The traditions between the two religions
were different, but both involved the covering of the head.

The cemetery was an amazing sight to see. Row after row of dif-
ferent-shaped tombstones were crammed together, many knocking
into each other, but all very old and very crumbly and very crooked.
One had a hard time imagining how there would have been room to
bury the bodies in such crowded quarters. It was nearly impossible to
walk between many of the tombs and was possible to see how some

may have risen from other layers as the earth had shifted through the years. So many lives were represented by all the tombstones. The numbers overwhelmed her.

Meredith left the cemetery in a slightly dizzy state and sat down on a bench outside its walls. Twelve thousand people, twelve thousand people who had all lived and died in this city were buried here. Where were all of these souls now? What had they accomplished? How many of them had been musicians like herself? How many of them were driven by passions during their lives like herself, only to experience them, live, and then die. How many of them had been poor, and why did their lives matter? Why did it matter if everyone would die? She thought of the wrinkled old face of Mother Teresa glowing with brilliance, love, and inner serenity. She was obviously near the time of her death, yet nothing but tranquility seemed to pass through her eyes, reaching the people she touched with a profound sense of purpose. There was no fear present. She seemed to know the secret. She seemed to hold the peace that would carry her to the next level of being. There had to be a next level of being. All of life had to have a purpose. There had to be a reason. Why would everyone be here if there were no reason?

She reached beneath her blouse and traced the outline of the Virgin on the medal Mother Teresa had given her. The Virgin had lived too, but she now was gone like the countless number of people in this cemetery. According to her Catholic belief, the Virgin was with God. It suddenly struck Meredith that they all had to be with God. For their lives to have meant anything, they all now had to be with God, somehow together in the same place. Jews, Catholics— they all took different paths to get there, but they all had to have reached the same destination at some point. And they were all somehow mysteriously woven together in some kind of whole. Mother Teresa radiated love. She seemed to have found the love of God and channeled it from God into her very being, then radiated it to others. Maybe that's what a saint was—someone who had found the love of God and lived through it on a daily basis, bringing it to others with joy and purpose.

Mother Teresa's mission was to share the love with the rest of the world that was so obsessed with things and power and money. She knew the answer to survival and she wanted to share it. It was that simple. It was that complicated, yet it was that simple: love. It was all about love—the giving and sharing of oneself with the rest of the world.

Meredith could think no more. She felt like she had just realized something vital to her being, something she had heard countless times but something her brain had never fully realized with meaning. It was there, plain as day, looking her in the eyes. But she could think no more. She started walking. She walked the sidewalks; she walked the streets; and she walked the cobblestones of Prague until her feet brought her to the river. She was at the Charles Bridge on the Vltava River.

Meredith began roaming the bridge, one of Prague's most famous bridges, once the only connection between Prague Castle and Old Town. Artists with their easels, musicians playing for meager contributions, and the stands of souvenir vendors lined both sides of the bridge, which today was a pedestrian bridge only. Shoulders bumped into shoulders at times due to the tremendous number of people who came to walk and drink in the scenic beauty of the river and the city. Constructed in 1357, the bridge was an impressive monument to the city. In the seventeenth century, statues, mostly of saints, began being placed on both sides of the bridge. The bridge was unique and beautiful. Meredith placed her elbows on the railing of the middle of the bridge and gazed out upon the murky brown waters below. Seagulls drifted by in search of food, trustingly ready to devour anything a passing tourist would throw at them, as white swans with their slender long necks huddled together along the banks of the river. Tour boats dotted the river, viewing the immense forest of tall green church spires and onion-shaped domes, separating the orangey red roofs of the ancient brown buildings. The personality and character of Prague was uniquely its own. It was an ancient treasure. And it had brought Meredith a new sense of how she viewed her life and its purpose.

Meredith slowly walked back to the hotel. She would grab a sandwich and a short nap to be ready for the excitement of the evening's rehearsal. She was looking forward to it all.

17

Music is the universal language of mankind.
—Henry Wadsworth Longfellow

Maria Braviak picked up Meredith early again so she could have her warm-up time and be ready. She once again complimented Meredith on her playing and then excused herself to do paperwork in her office. Much to Meredith's surprise, Paul Brennan appeared on the scene early, long before the other musicians arrived to unpack and warm-up. He looked handsome as ever, dressed in nice blue jeans, a gray turtleneck, and a gray tweed blazer reminiscent of the man from the airplane but in a different way. Somehow he didn't look seedy in his expensive blazer like the man from the airplane had looked in his. He looked sophisticated and handsome, with just a touch of gray speckling the sides of his dark hair. Tall and slender, he looked like he had a nice build under all of his expensive clothing. And he smelled good too! He appeared to be organizing the music on his music stand and then approached Meredith at the piano.

"Ms. Mason," he said smiling. "I can't begin to tell you how pleased we are with your interpretation of the Rachmaninoff. Your playing is strong and intense, as well as sensitive and sweetly mysterious. I appreciate your following my every nuance. Your attention to my every direction was impeccable, and I am immensely pleased with your work."

"Thank you, Dr. Brennan," replied Meredith. "I have great respect for your artistry as well. It was a great pleasure to work with a new conductor of your caliber."

"Now that we've exchanged compliments"—he laughed—"let me change the subject. During the afternoon, in your absence, I made an executive decision which I hope will please you. My only wish in doing this was that you leave here having experienced our culture to the fullest in the short amount of time that you are here." Meredith looked a bit puzzled as he went on but listened intently.

"I took the liberty of making dinner reservations for us for tomorrow night after rehearsal at a Czech restaurant on the edge of the city that presents dinner with Bohemian folk music, song, and dance. It is one of the only places of its kind I know of that combines authentic Czech music with traditional instruments from the past, highlighted by performing, costumed dancers. I invited Maria Braviak to join us, but she declined, saying she regretfully had other plans. I hope you will not misinterpret my invitation. My only wish is for you to experience the richness of the delightful culture that grew up here."

Meredith hesitated for a moment and then replied firmly with diligence, "Well, I certainly wouldn't want to leave here not having experienced the fullness of the culture, would I? I would be delighted to go, and I will look forward to it. Thank you for your kind concern. Sometimes executive decisions are necessary, aren't they?"

"Yes, they are." He smiled. He was obviously pleased that she had accepted his invitation.

"Then we will go following rehearsal, okay?"

"Okay." She smiled.

The musicians were beginning to enter and unpack. Paul Brennan went back to his music stand to prepare for the rehearsal. He began talking in Czech to two of the violinists who apparently had not pleased him with the way they had played a passage the evening before. He raised his voice, seeming a bit upset with them, which made her wonder if she had made the right decision about going to the restaurant. But not knowing the details of what had happened, she decided that all would be fine.

The rehearsal was magnificent once again. Meredith threw herself into the music and was totally swept away by the emotion of it all. She enjoyed herself immensely and found herself feverishly excited about performing the piece in front of an audience on Saturday evening. Paul Brennan was an exceptional conductor, and it was a privilege to be able to work with him, nonetheless being able to perform in such an amazing historical place as the Czech Republic. She loved what she did. She realized what a gift her connection to the music was and how most people never got to feel what she felt. She was given this gift. She worked all of her life using her abilities, but still they were a gift. She was opening the present and loving it!

She awoke Friday morning with renewed vigor. The jet lag was finally gone, and she looked forward with energy and enthusiasm to her last touring day and the upcoming concert. Deciding she would spend the time today visiting Prague Castle, she hoped to at least walk through the group of palaces, which was the largest coherent castle complex in the world made up of many different styles of architecture from Roman to Gothic. The complex stood across the river from Old Town, on the other side of the Charles Bridge, and dominated the skyline of Prague. In the center of the palace area rose the tall, pointed spires of St. Vitus Cathedral, whose vast stained-glass windows vividly and colorfully told of stories from the Bible. St. Wenceslas was buried there beneath the chapel dedicated to his memory, along with most of the other ancient Czech kings. Today the complex housed the living president of the Czech Republic.

Returning to the hotel midafternoon, she was pleased with all she had seen and done during her visit to the area. Tonight would be the icing on the cake. Being able to experience the culture of the Czech Republic through its folk music would be delightful. Going alone with Paul Brennan tonight might be another thing all together, but she was a big girl and knew she could take care of herself. His motives were probably totally innocent, but somehow his good looks and smooth manner of talking with her made her wonder if he had done this before. Placing a call to Evan before her nap, she decided not to mention where she was going that evening after rehearsal. Shoot. He didn't answer. Maybe that was best. She would speak to him tomorrow. After eating a bowl of soup from room service and being quite exhausted from the day's walk, sleep came easy.

Upon awaking, Meredith dressed in a sophisticated black Ralph Lauren pantsuit with a cream silk blouse and black spike heels. She piled her shiny long brown hair on top of her head, revealing the small silver earrings she loved wearing with all of her outfits.

Maria Braviak picked her up exactly on time, this being their final rehearsal before Saturday evening's concert. Paul Brennan did not arrive early as he had the night before, giving her lots of warm-up time. Musicians began arriving when Paul Brennan quietly walked up behind her and whispered, "You look lovely, my dear!"

She gave a brief "thank you" and thought, *Oh no, what have I done!*

18

Music is an outburst of the soul.
—Frederick Delius

Stepping upon the podium, Paul Brennan became his professional self. He demanded the most from every member of the orchestra during rehearsals and ran his rehearsals with a very professional manner. Players respected his musicianship and knew they had to come well prepared to each and every rehearsal. He quickly saw to it that anyone who didn't measure up to his high standards was immediately dismissed. There was no talking during his rehearsals. Everyone was expected to listen attentively and take correction with a positive attitude. He demanded polished musicianship, and he got it. On the other hand, he gave Meredith little correction. He seemed to know that the best way to get the most out of a soloist, who was a true artist, was to give her free reign with her craft. He could not have been more intuitive with Meredith. Her creativity and artistry thrived when she was free to express herself.

Once again, Meredith got into her playing with spirited enthusiasm. She played the best she had played that week. Maria Braviak sat alone in the center of the performing hall, smiling. She too was getting caught up in Meredith's playing. Under Paul Brennan's direction, Meredith and the orchestra became one, working together skillfully to reach new heights of musical magic. As the final chord sounded, Maria Braviak stood up, clapped loudly, and yelled, "Bravo!" Paul Brennan was obviously pleased and let the orchestra and Meredith know that he was. He gave a few final instructions for tomorrow's performance and then dismissed the group.

After putting on his coat jacket and gathering his music in his briefcase, he approached Meredith, dishing out glowing compliments. He quickly left his professional self behind and became the smooth social animal who had told her she looked lovely that evening. He and Meredith walked out to his car. He did not open her door for her, as Evan had always sweetly done. The absence of that made her think of Evan, wondering if she should be going out on a date with a handsome man halfway across the world.

"I hope you will drink in the loveliness of the city lit up at night as we cross the river. Prague is often said to be the most beautiful city in Europe. Her lights sparkle like diamonds on a fine piece of jewelry."

"I have been overwhelmed by the beauty of this city," Meredith replied, taking in the lights as they viewed the city from the bridge.

"Several bridges cross the river," Paul explained. "The Mánes Bridge is just one of many. The splendor of the lights from the bridges is like the splendor of your playing and the beauty of the one doing the playing."

Again, not knowing how to respond, she just quietly said, "Thank you." They drove without speaking for a few minutes and then Paul interrupted the silence.

"You will love this restaurant. The costuming of the dancers and the expertise of the musicians takes one to another era. Even being a classical musician, I can appreciate the spirit and flavor of the Bohemian tunes and the expertise with which they are played. You will as well."

As they entered the restaurant, they were led to their table through a room filled with long wooden tables covered with crisp white tablecloths. Warmly colored walls were decorated with gypsy scarves hanging as decorations. As they sat down, a waiter immediately came with a tray of shot glasses filled with a golden liquid.

"This," Paul joked, "is what I like to call fire water! If you drink it all, your eyes will dazzle like your playing, and happiness will fill your heart!" It was Becherovka, an aperitif manufactured and sold in the Czech Republic. Meredith took a small sip of the rich liquid, which was strong and sweet and warmed her insides on the way down. Paul laughed at her as he consumed his shot glass in one gulp. She did like the flavor but sipped on hers, as she was afraid to drink it too quickly.

"It will make you *strong like bull*," Paul teased again. Another waiter came filling all the glasses with wine. The wine was contained in a clear glass pitcher with a foot-long quarter-inch-wide clear glass spout. The wine shot out of the spout and went perfectly into each glass.

"Now that takes real talent." Meredith laughed. She saw that tonight had the makings of a merry evening! Then the music began.

"That piano-sized instrument is a cimbalom," explained Paul. It resembles the hammered dulcimer from Appalachia. And, yes, what you see over there is a Czech version of the bagpipe called the dudy."

"My goodness," Meredith exclaimed. "I never realized bagpipes existed anywhere else except in Great Britain."

"The violins, double bass, and sometimes a clarinet often finish out the ensemble," Paul continued.

A buxom female singer with a robust voice came out singing in Czech to the lively melodies of the ensemble. She was followed by gypsy dancers. The women were dressed in brightly colored skirts, ruffled white tops, and Bohemian scarves, and the men were wearing black pants and boots with long-sleeved red tops and colored scarves tied at the waist. The singing and the dancing and the stomping wrapped Meredith in the spirit of the culture; and she found herself enjoying the Becherovka, the wine, and laughing loudly. Paul seemed to be taking much pleasure from watching Meredith having a good time with the crowd of happy people. The Czech people knew how to have good time.

They were fed homemade breads; a nice vinegar-based salad; and potatoes, cabbage, and kielbasa, a traditional sausage. Warm plum strudel came for dessert, with coffee and tea. Then the polka music began for the people to join in.

"The polka is the most famous style of Bohemian music," Paul mentioned as he leaned toward Meredith.

"You will join me, won't you?"

"Oh, I don't know," Meredith said bashfully. But as more and more people went out to the dance floor, she gave in to his pleading. He took her hand, and they joined in on the fun. Paul was a good dancer. He led her through the polka as he led the orchestra through a piece of music, with vigor and gentle authority. She had learned the polka as a child from dancing at weddings, and followed his lead easily, having great fun as he twirled her around the dance floor. Then the ensemble began playing the waltz, and Paul and Meredith joined in gracefully, as if they had danced together all the time.

"The Viennese waltz is one of the most important Bohemian dance forms," added Paul as he spun her round and round to the graceful one, two, three of the music. As the waltz finished, they laughed with joy. Music and dancing were meant to go together, and being musicians, they both knew and felt the joy of combining them. They both admitted they were tired and went back to their table, having had a good time getting into the spirit of things.

"You are a wonderful dancer," Paul said, praising her skills on the dance floor. "Being the musician that you are, I would be surprised if you were not!"

"As a child, I learned to dance from my uncles when we attended weddings," Meredith replied. My uncle Tom was a magnificent dancer, and I learned by following his lead."

"And very nicely, I must add." Paul smiled at her with admiration. "Do you have a gentleman at home?" Paul asked gently.

"I do." Meredith smiled, relieved that he would ask.

"He is a very lucky one," Paul added, "to have captured the heart of someone like yourself." Again, she smiled bashfully.

"How about you?" Meredith asked, curious about his background.

"No," Paul replied. "I just have Maria Braviak to keep me in line. But she's just a friend and an exceptional business partner. We work together very well, and she is extremely efficient. I have a very satisfying life. My music keeps me happy."

"Yes," Meredith answered. I feel that way about my music too."

"I would like to invite you back to play another concert," Paul added, quickly changing gears from his social to his professional self.

"I know that tomorrow's concert will be an immense success. We are planning to do the Liszt piano concerto next season, and I would be pleased to have you as our soloist." Meredith's heart leapt with joy at the thought of actually coming back.

"I would be honored to return." Meredith smiled with obvious enthusiasm. "I have actually played the Liszt concerto with the Seattle Symphony."

"I know," Paul replied. "I have done my homework!" She smiled inside, realizing that he probably always did his homework with great diligence.

"I thought this would be my only visit to this beautiful city," Meredith added.

"Beautiful cities need beautiful people like yourself to fill them with excitement and joy," he complimented admirably. Meredith blushed and just took the compliment with a smile. "I will have Maria Braviak draw up the papers. You can sign them before you leave tomorrow."

"Thank you," Meredith said happily.

Before she left, she bought a bottle of Becherovka from one of the waiters walking around selling them, thinking that it would be a nice gift for Evan.

"I hope you're not planning to drink that all yourself." Paul laughed, making fun of her.

"No. It's a gift." She smiled.

Paul drove Meredith back to her hotel. He knew where she was staying since they had arranged her stay there.

"It has been a pleasure to share the evening with you, my dear," he said, taking her hand and kissing it gently. He held it a bit too long, making Meredith wonder for a moment what his motives were, but then he let it go.

"Thank you," Meredith said. "I had an incredible time. It was one of the highlights of my trip." He did not open the door for her as Evan had always done. She entered the hotel as he pulled away. *Wow,* Meredith thought, *what an evening.* It really was one of her favorite experiences of the week.

19

Where words leave off, music begins.

—Heinrich Heine

The next morning, she opened the heavy drapes to reveal a gorgeous sunny day. The buildings and church steeples of Prague seemed to be smiling at her. She had come to feel at home in this wonderful city of ancient buildings and winding cobblestone paths. The thought of leaving tomorrow meant the end of all she had experienced here. She would carry the memories with her forever, but the time here would be over after tonight's concert. A knock at the door startled her. After checking the peephole, she opened the door to reveal a smiling bellman holding a vase of a dozen red roses, which he seemed pleased to hand to her. He must have been imagining an admiring gentleman sending them to her. After tipping him and closing the door, she opened the card. It read, "I know you will play beautifully this evening. Know that you will be in my heart. Love, Evan." She picked up the phone and reached him this time on the first ring.

"Evan, I just received the roses. It was so sweet of you to send them. I will think of you as I play, and I will be wearing your medal."

"I know you'll do a magnificent job," Evan said lovingly.

"I wish I could be there to share the evening with you."

"Know that you will be in my heart as well," Meredith said honestly. But yet somehow it seemed like there was a great distance between them. She had experienced so much by herself and had thrived on it.

"I'll be at GSP to pick you up when you land. I can't wait to see you and hear all about the trip," Evan added.

"Evan, I can't begin to tell you how wonderful this whole week has been. And I've been invited back to do the Liszt Piano Concerto next season with the orchestra. I'm just spinning with excitement.

"I'm so very proud of you…so very proud," Evan said honestly, with a slight bit of sadness in his voice that Meredith did not pick up on through the static in the telephone. Meredith said goodbye and shed a tear or two. Evan could not be any sweeter.

As Evan hung up, the worry of the possibility of losing her to all of this glamour and excitement hung heavy in his heart. He merely had simplicity and love to offer her compared to the sparkle and glitter of the international performing world. He had little money and no recognition in his profession. He couldn't give her fancy clothes, fancy houses, or fancy trips to exotic places. He could only shower her with his love. The choice would be hers to make. He could offer love and commitment. Would that be enough after what she had begun to experience?

20

Music is to the soul what words are to the mind.

—Modest Mussorgsky

Maria Braviak had arranged for Meredith to receive a total spa treatment at the hotel that afternoon so she would be relaxed and refreshed for the evening's performance. She would have an hour's massage and a facial, followed by a manicure and a pedicure. What a relaxing treat! She enjoyed the usual yummy brunch at the restaurant and then went immediately for her treatment. Having several people caring for her every need was pure delight. Any tightness or stiffness present in her muscles was gone, and she felt like a princess being waited on by her maidens. Totally being the center of attention was a whole new world for her. It was really quite nice.

After napping and enjoying a bowl of soup and crackers from room service, she showered and began dressing for the evening's concert. Room service had cleaned and pressed her gown and had it hanging in the closet, waiting and ready for her to wear. It was fall in the Czech Republic, and the alluring rust-colored gown of silky fabric she had worn in the Spartanburg concert would be perfect for her European debut. The leaves were changing, and the temperature was crisp. It would be an amazing evening. Meredith took the medals of St. Christopher and the Virgin Mary and attached them to the inside of her bra with a safety pin. She wanted St. Christopher, Mary, and especially the spirit of Mother Teresa to be with her on this momentous occasion. With the three of them close to her heart, things could only go well. As always, she piled her long silky hair on top of her head, fastened the small silver earrings in place, and slipped on her gown.

Maria Braviak met Meredith in the lobby and smiled widely with approval as she saw how lovely Meredith looked. Other guests looked on, wondering who the Cinderella princess was and where she was going. They quickly entered a waiting car and drove off.

Maria Braviak took Meredith to a soundproof room deep in the bowels of the performing venue, telling her she would have an hour and a half to warm-up and relax. Before she could get into her preconcert routine, Paul Brennan knocked on the door and entered. He looked stunningly handsome in his black tuxedo, with his dark hair accented by a bit of silvering at the temples. He was tall and well-built. He would be an amazing catch for any woman.

"My dear, I cannot begin to share with you what is going through my mind as I gaze at you standing before me, looking so incredibly beautiful as you do. You will capture the hearts of all the gentlemen in the audience before you even begin to perform." He walked over to her slowly and held both of her hands in his and then took her right hand and gently kissed it. "I came to wish you well. We will make beautiful music together this evening," he remarked, perhaps intending more than one meaning to his comment. He stood just a bit too close to her, making her feel a bit uncomfortable. He feverishly stared into her eyes for a moment with a gleam of devilish intent and then turned and left. As he reached the door, he looked back and said, "Go out and capture the hearts of your audience. You have already captured mine!"

As he left, she felt as if the wind had been knocked out of her. She didn't know what to think or feel. She had never been romanced with such a polished routine. And yes, it felt like a routine. It felt like maybe he had done this before. She couldn't think about it now. She began her preperformance warm-ups and pushed Paul Brennan and his advances out of her head. She was good at focusing only on her music. That was what she did.

It was time. This was it. This was her European debut. This was what she had dreamed of doing for a lifetime, and now the moment had arrived. The venue was dark, as bright lights sparkled down upon the orchestra. All was perfectly quiet as everyone waited. The tall, slender girl with the striking good looks and sparkling talent entered the stage to thunderous applause. She stood tall and radiated confidence as she walked. The sight of the magnificent hall filled with clapping, animated people filled her heart with pure excitement. She was ready. She purposefully did not look at Paul Brennan as she entered and took her place at the large Steinway in front of the orchestra. Pure silence filled the hall as the audience anticipated the excitement that was about to begin. After sitting for a moment to focus and compose herself, she nodded at Paul and began.

She took command of the music immediately as she always did. The bold beginning of the Rachmaninoff made it easy to begin with strength and pure control. The orchestra and piano immediately blended together in sound and spirit under the expert direction of Paul Brennan. Everyone in the room was immediately united with Meredith and the orchestra which expertly swept them away on a magic carpet of sound. There was not an unfocused eye in the hall as the piece proceeded with the boldness and the sweetness and the majesty the composer had intended to create. Meredith and Paul held the magic together until the final chord of the piece resounded through the hall. It was finished. It had been magnificent.

Meredith played "Claire de Lune" for her encore, followed by a standing ovation and the sounds of people yelling and screaming for more. She was given the customary dozen red roses and had tears streaming down her face as she left the stage. She had beautifully pulled off her European debut, assuring the continuation of her professional career as a concert pianist. Her artistry would now be recognized by the international musical community. She would have a stamp of approval on her future.

The concert finished with the orchestra playing "The Radetzky March," a piece by Johann Strauss senior that was loved by Europeans in general. People began doing the traditional handclap about halfway through the piece, which ended with everyone leaving in a good mood.

Still frozen and immobilized just slightly off stage by the realization of what she had just accomplished, and drowning herself in tears of happiness, Meredith received a big bear hug from Paul as he came bounding off the stage with a huge smile on his face.

"You captured not only their hearts but also their souls," he praised as he hugged her again with pure delight. A few higher-ups in the music world came backstage immediately to meet Meredith and to give Paul their sincere congratulations, not only on the concert but also upon having selected Meredith as his soloist. She was basically unknown in the international music world, but that would soon change, as word of her stunning performance would travel through the upper music circles of the world. Her name would now be recognized, her future guaranteed. After all of the handshaking was over and the last of the well-wishers had left, Paul turned to Meredith smiling, again revealing his pride and praise of her playing.

21

Where words leave off, music begins.
—Hans Christian Andersen

"Y ou must come out with me for a congratulatory drink. I can't just let you go like this, out into the night, without at least a chance to say goodbye."

"Oh, I don't know," she stammered, not knowing what to say. "I have an early flight to catch tomorrow morning."

"I insist…just one drink," he pleaded.

"Then we will part happily until the next time." She finally reluctantly agreed that one drink wouldn't hurt, and she went to gather up her things. It wasn't the drink she was worried about. It was the thought of what might come with it.

Maria Braviak found her to offer her congratulations, and Meredith thanked her sincerely for all that she had done to make her trip a pleasant one. Not knowing whether to say anything, Maria Braviak finally confronted Meredith.

"Ms. Mason," she started. "Paul is a wonderful conductor and a fine person, but he has a taste for pretty women. Just be careful so you don't wind up getting yourself hurt."

With that said, Meredith replied, "Thank you, Maria. I appreciate your advice. My only intention was to be polite and not offend his pride in offering the invitation." Maria Braviak nodded sincerely and then was gone. Not knowing how to take all of this, Meredith was glad that Maria had intervened with a bit of advice.

Paul took her to the Lavka Bar and Club on the River Vltava next to the Charles Bridge.

"Come with me," he insisted, taking her hand. She followed him, and he led her out to the wooden deck that protruded over the banks of the river.

"The sparkling lights of last night are now the diamond jewels surrounding us as we stand here. That is Prague Castle, immediately across the river, dressed like a lady in her finest attire." Despite the chill of the fall air, the view was stunning. The dark, rippling waters of the Vltava lapped gently on the shoreline as seagulls and pigeons were still flying about, trying to catch bits of bread and food the tourists were still tossing off the Charles Bridge. All four of the bridges in view were lit up. People riding by on dinner cruises stood on the upper decks of their boats, taking in the magnificence of the scenery.

"Here, let me keep you warm," he offered as he took off his coat jacket and wrapped it around her shoulders. She could not refuse the warmth of the jacket, but his arm around her shoulder and the gentle squeeze that came with it was a bit of an unwanted surprise.

"Paul," she eluded.

"You do know that I have someone at home, don't you?"

"Yes, I'm aware of that," he replied.

"But a woman as lovely as yourself deserves to be attended to when she is far from home by herself in a strange city. I mean no harm. I just want to see that you are being cared for."

"Thank you," she responded, being glad that she had been assertive enough to state her feelings. It was he who then changed the subject.

"Let's go inside and get a drink. What may I get for you?" Meredith ordered a red wine while Paul had scotch and water. He also ordered a plate of hors d'oeuvres with various soft and hard cheeses, cold meats, and olives.

"Everyone needs a second dinner at this hour," he joked.

"This is lovely," Meredith added.

"I usually only eat a small amount on the evenings when I'm due to perform, so I'm actually a little hungry."

"A wise decision," he agreed. They sat at a small table on the edge of the dance floor, watching the people enjoying themselves dancing. The music was neither folk nor classical. It was what you would hear in an American bar on a normal evening.

"So tell me, what does your gentleman do?"

"He's a musician," Meredith replied. "He is a cello player. He also teaches calculus at a local college."

"Ah, a cello player," Paul remarked. "The cello is one of the more romantic instruments of the orchestra. No wonder he was able to capture the heart of such a beautiful woman!"

Meredith got the strong feeling that this handsome man with the smooth manner would have hit on her if she had not talked about Evan with such feeling.

All at once he purposefully changed the subject, becoming the professional conductor that he was. "We shall be delighted to have you join us next season for a return engagement. It will most likely be in late summer or early fall. Maria will be in touch soon when the schedule is finalized."

"This will be very exciting for me. I will look forward to returning," Meredith added. "I have fallen in love with this city. It will be an added bonus to be able to come back." Paul nodded.

"I expect you will soon be receiving many more offers when word gets around about your success here. You are a very talented young woman. Your career opportunities can only improve from this point on."

"I hope so," added Meredith!

"I know so!" Paul smiled. "May I order you another glass of wine?"

"Thank you, but no," Meredith replied. "I have an early flight in the morning, so I really need to get back to the hotel. Thank you for everything. You have been a wonderful conductor to work under. Working with you has been an amazing professional experience. You have given me many new insights into my playing, and I am grateful for the experience."

"My pleasure," Paul replied. "I will look forward to your return."

Paul drove her to her hotel, and this time, he did get out and open the door for her. He took her hand and kissed it gently. "Until next time." He smiled.

"Yes, thank you," Meredith replied. She waved goodbye as he got in his car and drove off.

Meredith stroked the silhouettes of St. Christopher and Mary as she rode up alone in the elevator. They had experienced her success with her. She again remembered the love radiating from the eyes of Mother Teresa. It was the love that all people were meant to find and cherish in this lifetime. She felt she had only experienced the tip of it all in her life so far. There was so much more. Mother Teresa seemed to have found all of it in this lifetime, or at least she knew where to find it. She seemed to know the answer.

22

Music produces a kind of pleasure which
human nature cannot do without.

—Confucius

The huge jetliner powerfully rose up into the clouds, leaving the orangey, red roofs of the farmhouses surrounding the city of Prague in the distance. The beauty of Prague and the Czech Republic would soon be only a memory in the chambers of her mind. She watched out the window as the houses and barns and trees became mere dots in the colored landscape below. Billowy white clouds began to cover the landscape, slowly at first in wisps and then in big cotton-like gobs. Then the land was gone. The plane made its usual up-and-down bounces as it gained height and speed quickly, approaching its cruising altitude. Once achieved, the flight attendants began moving about the cabin, serving drinks and preparing dinner. The flight would go straight to Atlanta, and then Meredith would take a connecting flight to GSP. Now that she had left, she was anxious to be going home. She would see Evan. She had experienced all of this without the presence of his smile or the warmth of his company. Despite all the new experiences she had had on her own, she realized she had missed him terribly. He was a piece of the puzzle, an important piece. But she wondered how she would fit the pieces together to make a whole.

Following the trip across the ocean to Atlanta, the flight to GSP took a mere fifteen minutes flying time. The plane basically went up and then started descending right after cruising altitude was reached. After flying over the familiar chain restaurants on I-85 and the tall rows of loblolly pines lining the interstate, they touched down on the tarmac smoothly and routinely. There had been nothing of a routine nature in this trip for Meredith. It had been the culmination of a dream built upon years of hard work and effort. Tears of joy slowly started rolling down her face as she reached inside her blouse to rub the figures of St. Christopher and Mary that hung from the chain Evan had given her. They had accompanied her on her epic journey. She was home! Memories blurred and visions of the country so far away that she had come to love so very much in only a week's time were temporarily frozen. She realized he would be waiting. He would be standing there anticipating her embrace, the scent of her hair, and the warmth of her laughter. She thought of his dimpled smile, his sandy brown hair, and the way he looked at her through eyes, hungry for more. And then she saw him standing at the front of the waiting people, tall and slender and amazingly handsome in his jeans and turtleneck sweater. She began running, her heart beating faster, as she flew into his waiting arms, accepting the strong force of his hug and the hungry delight of his kisses despite all those who surrounded them, watching the reunion with smiles of envy. "Meredith, my Meredith!" He began stroking her silky hair, holding on to her, not wanting to let go. She stood still and accepted all of it with joyful glee.

"I have missed you so much. So incredibly much," he blurted out, not caring who heard or who watched.

"I know. I really do know," said Meredith in a slightly more subdued tone.

"It is so good to be here with you!" Holding hands like two teenagers, they almost skipped to the baggage claim area. They drove to Spartanburg with her head on his shoulder and his arm around hers. The warmth of their closeness fueled their longing for each other.

Once inside the picture-perfect bungalow on Palmetto Street, Evan stared at her with eyes full of love and longing. He unbuttoned her trench coat and let it slide from her shoulders to the floor. He pulled her close to him with warm hugs and tender kisses. Slowly he backed her up to the couch and sat her down, pressing her close to his chest, hungrily enjoying the hugs and kisses he had waited for all week long. She kissed him back, accepting the softness and warmness of his touch. He stopped and looked straight in her eyes with love and devotion pouring out.

"You are beautiful," he said, stroking her hair and shoulders, looking intently at her angelic face.

"I love you, I truly love you. You don't need to say anything. I just wanted to tell you. I've longed to tell you. Now you know, and that's all we need to say for now." He pulled her close to him, and she rested her head on his shoulder, with his arms around her. There, in the security of his embrace, exhaustion and jet lag caught up with her, and she fell soundly asleep at his side.

Ever so gently, Evan lifted her up and carried her to her bedroom. He placed her sleeping head on the pillow and pulled the warm down comforter over her slender silhouette. Closing her door, he propped up the pillows on the sofa and made a bed for himself for the night. She was safely home. He felt at peace.

Meredith woke up the next morning to the delightful smell of bacon cooking in the kitchen. Getting out of bed, she noticed she still had on her traveling outfit from the day before. By the time on the clock, she realized she must have been asleep for over twelve hours. Her body had no sensation of what time it should be right now. Jet lag had completely taken over. In the kitchen, Evan was hard at work, determined to show off his culinary skills. With a spatula in one hand, looking like a male Julia Child clad in a white apron, he smiled at her.

"Hi, stranger. I thought the smell of food would wake you up!" She went to the counter and poured herself a mug of steaming hot coffee and then pulled up a chair.

"I'm starving!"

Evan poured the already scrambled eggs into a buttered frying pan and pushed down the button on the toaster. "You passed out on me last night shortly after we got here. You were totally out of it!"

Meredith looked apologetically at him. "I'm so sorry. I had so much to tell you and wanted to share it all, and then the exhaustion of the past two days just got to me."

Evan looked at her seductively as he finished scrambling the eggs. "I did enjoy the part of your homecoming we did get to share though," he added. "It was very nice."

She looked at him with alarm in her eyes. "Nothing happened that I don't remember, did it?"

Evan dished out the bacon and eggs and toast. He would have loved to play with her mind, but instead, he answered honestly. "No, no, don't worry that you missed something! You were just so nice and cuddly and warm and you did make me wish that you hadn't fallen asleep on me."

"Oh."

He got the butter and jelly out of the fridge and sat down next to her. She pulled out the chain he had given her with the St. Christopher medal on it and showed him the medal of the Virgin Mary.

"Mother Teresa was on our plane going to Rome. She gave me this medal!"

"Holy crap," Evan exclaimed, and then apologized profusely. "Pardon my French, but you actually got to meet Mother Teresa?"

Meredith related the whole story to him about Mother Teresa from beginning to end. She told him about her eyes and the love that radiated from them, filling her soul. Evan rubbed his finger over the raised figure of the Virgin on the medal, just as Meredith had been compelled to do all during her journey. He sat in awe of what she had told him. They talked for another hour, and then Evan admitted sadly that he had a class to teach that afternoon in Asheville, but that he had enough time to quickly help her clean up.

"Thanks, for the breakfast, Evan. It hit the spot."

"My pleasure," he added. He took both her hands and kissed her on the cheek. "I'll call later. I know you need to get settled. See you soon!"

"Bye," she echoed as he slipped out the door.

The first step was to wash everything that came out of her suitcase. The gown would go to the cleaners, to be ready for the next time. The next time. She wasn't certain when that would be, but she felt like she had definitely started something by doing this concert abroad. The week had been amazing. It was like her life was in a different gear now, going at record speed to who knows where. But it was good to be home. And it was so good to be with Evan again.

The phone rang, and it was Bill Preston. Meredith had expected his congratulatory call, but following his high praise of her and her artistry, he delivered some heartbreaking news. Helen Preston was in the hospital. They were still in the process of diagnosing her, but they suspected it was some kind of blood disorder, perhaps leukemia. He would not be in today and told Meredith to please take the day off too to get over her jet lag before returning to her full schedule. He said she should wait to visit perhaps another day until things were more under control. Meredith asked if there was anything she could do, and he simply said, "Pray."

After hanging up, Meredith reached inside her sweatshirt and stroked the figures of the two medals that had been hanging there together over the past week. She wanted to pray, but it had been years, if ever, that praying had been a part of her life. Her mother had taken her to church as a little girl, but that had all stopped as she grew older. She had no conception of prayer or how to pray, but after having experienced the love and peace that Mother Teresa radiated, she knew she wanted to personally find that place of great serenity where Mother Teresa found her center.

23

Music will help dissolve your perplexities and purify
your character and sensibilities, and in time of care and
sorrow, will keep a fountain of joy alive in you.
—Dietrich Bonhoeffer

So far, Meredith's whole center of being had been her music. It had
served her well and had satisfied the deep yearning for fulfillment
that had always been within her. It had covered up the hole left inside
her by her parent's passing. Despite experiencing that tragedy, she
was happy and pleased with her life. But was there something more
she was missing?

After showering and grabbing the things that needed to go to
the cleaners, Meredith jumped in her VW bug and headed downtown to the historic small church nestled amongst the trees on a
street near the center of town.

St. Paul's Church, tiny as it was, had a presence all of its own,
with its clay-colored stucco exterior, striking stained glass windows,
and tall green spire pointing upwardly to the heavens. She could picture it sitting among the buildings of Prague. It was that unique.
Despite the fact that it was the middle of October, the church still
had flowers blooming outside around it. That struck Meredith as
being odd as she opened one of the heavy wooden doors leading
inside.

The church was peacefully dark inside with the only light being
the rays of the sun trying to peek through the stained glass windows.
Dark-stained wooden wainscoting rose halfway up the walls, matching the rows of old dark-stained pews that sat in silence. Calming
light-blue-green walls led to the intricately carved floor to ceiling

wood behind the marble altar with a massive wooden cross holding the crucified body of Christ. A lantern emitting candlelight shining through red glass hung from a long chain on the left side of the altar. The peaceful silence was broken only by the unrhythmic occasional creaking of the old wood that was everywhere throughout the sanctuary. Even the tall ceiling that rose to a point above the center aisle was lined with dark-stained wooden boards supported by heavy inside buttressing. The smell of incense was everywhere, perhaps still lingering from a previous service. The atmosphere was peaceful, gentle, and evoked memories of the serenity she had experienced in Mother Teresa's presence.

A tall statue of the Virgin Mary hung on the left front altar, with her hands folded in prayer, as her head bowed in reverence. Meredith stared at the statue of Mary. She reached for her medal hanging from the chain around her neck. On the back of the medal were the hearts of Jesus and Mary, Jesus's crowned with thorns, and Mary's pierced with a sword. Meredith thought of how excruciatingly painful it must have been for Mary to watch silently as the child she had carried in her womb, the child she had raised and given her love to, was slaughtered and killed like an animal. For a moment, she empathized with Mary, feeling the horror of the pain she had experienced as the Mother of Jesus. She walked to the altar, knelt down, and lit a candle in the rack of candles in front of the Virgin.

She prayed for Helen Preston in her own words, holding the medal in her hands as she prayed from her heart. She left quietly, with the occasional creaking of the wooden beams being the only sound interrupting the silence.

She returned to school the next day and was flooded with faculty and students alike coming to her studio to ask about Prague and her concert debut there. Her students, especially, spent most of their lesson time wanting to know all about her trip, and she sacrificed lesson time to personally relate the details to satisfy their curiosity. Little was known about Helen Preston's health, and Meredith's heart broke as she thought of the immense pain and stress their family must be going through at this time. The Prestons were only in their early fifties, and that seemed too young for them to have to deal with disease and suffering of that magnitude. Evan called, and after relaying to him the details of the Prestons, he said he would bring dinner that evening, and maybe they could pay a visit to the hospital. Delighted not to have to eat alone, she welcomed the idea and said she would love to visit the hospital with him that evening. She hung up and then thought about having to face the possibility of the death of someone she knew. She had buried the experience of her parent's death deep within her soul. Would she have the strength to deal with this again so soon?

24

There is nothing in the world so much like prayer, as music is.
—William P. Merrill

Meredith had a gap of time between her last two lessons. She sat down at the piano and began playing a Brahms etude. Heartbreaking, empathetic feelings of concern, worry, and pain became woven into the music she poured out into the room. The opening of the wound of her parents' death joined her concerns about the Prestons. Lifeless black notes were energized, becoming a soothing tonic for the hurt that filled Meredith's spirit. She lost all awareness of time and space and became part of her music as it consoled her and expressed the heartache she could not put into words. Her hair flew loosely, back and forth through the air, as she immersed herself deeper and deeper into the soulful melodies that became powerful medicine for her wounded spirit.

A knock at the door announced the presence of her last student for the day. She composed herself and tried to give all her attention to the deserving student, despite the feelings still raging within her. After finishing the lesson, she jumped in her car and once again drove to the little Catholic church in the center of town as she had done the day before. Before leaving her car, she reached for the chain around her neck that held her two precious medals and stroked the outline of the figure of the Virgin on the medal given to her by Mother Teresa. This medal, along with the medal of St. Christopher given to her by Evan, had been her constant companion.

She opened the heavy wooden doors of the church, entering into the stillness, silence, and mostly darkness of the building. The church was again filled with the scent of incense that created a peaceful mood of prayer. The church was old. She thought of all the people from the past who had offered up their prayers here to a God in heaven she felt she barely knew. People who had prayed, lived their lives, and then passed on had come here looking for answers to the same questions that had filled her mind so much in the past few weeks. Like the Jewish graveyard, and Prague itself, this church was a holy place. It was a place of the past, where people of the present were living out their lives trying to find answers to the eternal questions of the meaning of life and what it led to. People like the Prestons, suffering from disease and other problems, came searching for answers. People came searching for peace amidst the uncertainness of life. They were people in search of what Mother Teresa seemed to have found. She took out the prayer card she had from Prague and prayed the prayer it contained for Helen Preston.

"Remember, most gracious Virgin Mary, that never was it known, that anyone who fled to thy protection, implored thy help, or sought thy intercession was left unaided. Inspired with this confidence I fly unto thee, o Virgin of virgins, my Mother. Oh Mother of the word incarnate, despise not my petitions but in thy mercy, hear and answer me, amen." She read over the words of the prayer again to herself. It said, "Never was it known." It didn't just ask for help. It said that anyone who prayed and asked for help would not be left unaided. Help would never be denied. That was a powerful statement.

While she was praying and contemplating the meaning of the prayer she had just said, a door on the altar creaked as it opened, and an old priest wearing a long black cassock appeared, seeming to check the tabernacle. He knelt down at the altar and prayed. When finished, he blessed himself and came to sit in the pew in front of Meredith.

"Welcome, my dear. I am Father Flanagan. I do not want to intrude, but I saw you here yesterday as well as today. Something must be weighing heavily on your heart. Sometimes it helps to share your concerns with another. I would be most happy to offer my help in any way that I can." Meredith saw the love in his eyes and could sense that he was a man of prayer and that she could trust him.

"Hello, Father. I am Meredith Mason. Thank you for your concern." She shared her worry for Helen Preston and then went on to tell him about her encounter with Mother Teresa, the medal, and the prayer card. She told him that she had been away from the church for years and that she was searching for the meaning and peace that seemed to radiate from the small but powerful presence of Mother Teresa.

"That is a lot for one person to carry in her heart, my dear," he went on. "Your search for the meaning of life is commendable, as well as the empathetic concern for your friend's health. We all have some kind of cross to bear in this lifetime. God never gives anyone a cross they cannot bear. With every cross, he always sends the grace with which to bear it."

He paused, thought, and then continued on. "Mary's prayer states that never has anyone who has approached her with sincerity been left unaided. Prayer is answered by God through the intercession of Mary, his most holy Mother. God does not always answer our prayers in the way that we would wish or in the time frame that we would want, but he does hear and answer every prayer. We must have confidence that he is there through every tribulation and that he lovingly cares what happens to us. In meeting Mother Teresa, you have been blessed with the privilege of having met a living saint. Not everyone is blessed with a privilege like this. God loves you very much to have shared her with you, even if just for a moment. And reasonably so, you are correct to realize that he wants this experience to change your life in some way. God often does his work through our encounters with other people. Mother Teresa has found her center in God and is a perfect role model for us all. God is most likely wanting this for you and for every one of us. You are fortunate to be realizing this so early in your lifetime. Many people die never realizing this."

Meredith just sat quietly, impressively touched by all that he was saying. "I will pray for you, my dear, and for your friend, Mrs. Preston."

Meredith looked at him with great respect. "Thank you, Father. You have helped a lot." She paused, trying to think how to best express the rest of her desires and then finally just blurted them out. "I want to learn to pray so I may have the peace and serenity that Mother Teresa beholds."

He gently smiled. "My dear, you do not have to recite any fancy words to pray to God our Father. The best prayers are the words that come from our hearts. God sees the words that are in our hearts. You please him by sharing yourself with him openly and honestly. There is nothing you cannot tell him. You are his child. He only wants to love you like a Father. Go now in peace, and take his love with you, sharing it with everyone you meet. That pleases Him the most. And remember, I am always here for you to talk with, if the need arises."

Meredith thanked him for his help. He turned and quietly left the sanctuary. Meredith said the prayer once more and then left the stillness and silence of the church, broken only by the occasional unrhythmic creaking of the wooden boards.

25

Music is the shorthand of emotion.

—Leo Tolstoy

She went back home and feverishly began playing the Rachmaninoff with all the emotions and feelings that were churning inside of her. Her music raged with fire and intensity that calmed and comforted her as she sorted out the thoughts and feelings swirling in her brain. Why did bad things happen to good people? Why did the world have to be sprinkled with bad things at all? What did it all mean? The sound of her feelings expressed on the piano pounded the walls of her little bungalow as she poured forth what painfully lie in her heart.

Evan arrived at six o'clock with meatloaf dinners from Wade's, a local restaurant that specialized in home-cooked meals at an affordable price. Meat loaf, mashed potatoes with gravy, and Southern turnip greens were the perfect comfort foods to sooth away troubles from the soul, along with yeast rolls and sweet tea, of course. The two gobbled up their dinners eagerly, talking little but feeling the sorrow of the moment.

After stopping at the grocery store for some fresh flowers in a vase, they found Helen Preston's room in the north tower of the huge medical center in downtown Spartanburg. They were pleased to see Dr. Preston there. Helen Preston seemed to be sleeping peacefully. Bill Preston rose when he saw them in the doorway, took the flowers, and motioned to them to come out in the hall.

"How very nice of you both to come. I greatly appreciate it, and Helen would too if she were awake." Bill Preston appeared nervous and tired to Meredith. He was usually a pillar of strength at the college, totally in control of everything; but tonight, she saw a fragile and vulnerable side to him that she had never seen before.

"Helen had been running a high fever for two days," he began, getting almost teary eyed as he spoke about it. His love and affection for her was obvious as he continued. "We couldn't get the fever down, and then she began bleeding from the nose and becoming short of breath. She complained that she was aching all over. I didn't know what to do. It was midnight, and things were getting progressively worse. I brought her to the emergency room here, and they admitted her when they realized the fever was not going to break. It's not flu. They are testing her for some kind of leukemia." His voice cracked as he said this. He almost seemed to be shaking with worry.

Meredith wanted to hug him, so she did. He hugged her back, welcoming the comfort it gave him as he made a valiant effort to hold back the tears. It was pitiful to see this energetic big, tall man going to pieces at the sight of his wife in a hospital bed.

Meredith asked if they could do anything at the college, and he said no, that his schedule had been cancelled until further notice. "If there's anything," Meredith said, "anything we can do, please don't hesitate to ask. I mean that sincerely." He thanked her with another hug and left them standing there as he went back to his post in the chair at her bedside.

Meredith couldn't speak as she and Evan left the hospital. Then she began rambling as they drove home. "We all think we have everything under control. We take credit for everything that we accomplish and pretend that all of our success is of our own doing, and then something like this comes along and knocks us off our pedestal, making us realize that we really have control over very little. It's like my playing. I take credit for it all, but then it could be taken from me in the blink of an eyelid. Life is so fragile. We never realize this until what we thought what was ours is taken away from us." She thought of her parents. She thought of how they had been taken from her without notice or preparation and how she had blamed herself for their death. They were gone. Gone forever never to be seen again.

Her rambling stopped as she realized that that was what she was doing. Evan realized her need to get it all out and made no comments as she poured out all of her confused feelings. They reached the house in silence, and Evan walked her to her door.

"I'll come in if you like, or I'll leave you with your thoughts, if that's what you prefer." Meredith smiled. Evan was always so thoughtful and considerate of her and her feelings.

"Thanks, Evan. I think I'd just rather be alone for a bit and get to bed early." He kissed her gently on the cheek.

"Don't worry. Your worrying will not change the outcome of things. Get some rest." He smiled and drove off into the night.

The next morning, she had a memo in her school mailbox waiting for her from her agent. The artistic director of the Chicago Symphony had heard of her success in Prague from Maria Braviak and wanted to schedule her to play on next year's calendar. Normally she would have gone over the edge with excitement, but today she just took the note and headed down the hallway toward her studio. On the way, she passed another faculty member who inquired about Dr. Preston's wife. She told him all she knew and continued on her way. Feeling down all day, she tried to appear upbeat for her students but had a hard time trying to pretend that everything was fine when she was hurting inside. How could something like this happen to the Prestons. Things like this were supposed to happen to other people, not to the people you knew and loved. Between lessons, she called her agent to give him the go-ahead to schedule something for next year with the Chicago Symphony, lacking her usual luster and buoyancy. Even he noticed that something was wrong. She had the concert with the San Francisco Symphony coming up in late November after Thanksgiving. She would be busy, but that was how she preferred to live her life.

Being busy covered up the hurt that life had given her. It was therapeutic. Her music was therapeutic. Why did she have to suffer the hurt that life had bestowed upon her?

26

God loves each of us, as if there was only one of us.

—St. Augustine

Following her last lesson, she made the short drive to the little church in the center of town. She pulled open the heavy wooden door and was glad that there was no one inside. She went up and took her regular seat in the front of the church. Salty tears rolled down her face as she silently poured out her feelings and prayers in her own words, receiving comfort from just being there, knowing and feeling that there really was a God who was listening to her. Lighting a candle at the foot of the altar, she returned to her pew and meditated about why she was here on earth, why everyone was here, and why her presence here and the presence of others would have mattered after everyone was gone. When the wooden door on the altar opened with a creak, she had no idea how long she had been there. Father Flanagan said his usual prayers, kneeling at the altar, and then came and sat in front of Meredith. Seeing him made a few more salty tears roll down her face, a happening which she tried to hide with the quick wipe of a tissue.

"My dear," he started, "you seem to be very agitated today. If I can help in any way, I would be most grateful to do so."

She related Mrs. Preston's condition to him and remarked how fragile life was and how what we so idly took for granted could be changed in an instant. She added that she couldn't see the meaning of it all, if it could be extinguished in a moment like putting the fire out on a candle. Had the brightness of the candle meant anything once it was out?

Father Flanagan took a deep breath before he began, "My dear, you carry the weight of the world on your shoulders. You are pondering questions that have been asked through the ages by many souls who have lived throughout history. Who am I, a mere priest, to answer these questions? But I will try to give you the best direction that I can." She smiled, drying another tear with her tissue.

"We all live here together. Our lives are like the ripples of a stone thrown into a pond of water. We have no idea how far the ripples go or who they touch as they move outward. What we have accomplished with our life may affect other people in ways that we will never fully realize. That is the beauty of it all. God uses people to spread his love in the world to other people. He works through people, the way he brought his love to you through Mother Teresa. We are all holy, every last one of us, in that we are instruments of God. God even uses the bad deeds people do to influence others. If we lead a good life, it will influence others in a positive manner. Those of us who are fortunate enough, that through prayer and meditation, realize there is more to experience once we leave this lifetime behind, are blessed with a sense of purpose regarding what we do here, no matter how long or how short our time here on earth is or how happy or heartbreaking it may be. We have a loving Father. A loving Father would never give his child something bad. Hard as it is to trust him sometimes, we must know that all that we experience here on earth is for our eternal good. It is meant to make us whole. If we know that, then there is no reason to be anxious or afraid or to worry about anything that happens to us. It is all happening under the watchful eye of a loving Father, who has more planned for us beyond our life here. It all has meaning. We must trust that this meaning will be revealed to us at some point in time, but perhaps not in this lifetime. It's all about faith. And we develop that faith through prayer."

Meredith just listened in astonishment to the wisdom of the words this old man was sharing with her. She felt privileged that he would share himself and his experience of his faith with her in this manner.

"I have someone I want you to meet." If I could arrange it, do you think you could meet me here tomorrow at this time? There is someone in St. Theresa's Nursing Home across the street who I would like you to meet." Meredith thought this was a strange request but then decided to appease this holy man who had helped her so much with her feelings.

"I would be honored to go with you, Father. I can meet you here at the same time tomorrow." Father Flanagan nodded, stood, and then left through the squeaky altar door. Meredith's mind was spinning. She was having trouble holding on to and comprehending all that he had said to her. It was like he had presented the wisdom of the world to her in a few minutes' time.

Meredith called Evan when she got home and tried to share with him her conversation with Father Flanagan but had trouble relating it to Evan the way that Father had related it to her. Evan listened quietly to all she said. He had little to add to comfort her with, but just knowing he was listening was soothing. Evan was incredibly sweet. He had all the thoughtful concern and empathy that anyone could want in a really good friend. His caring was real. As she hung up, she felt confused and upset about the misfortunes the Prestons were going through right now. How fortunate she was to have met Father Flanagan at this time in her life. It was like he just appeared when she needed to hear what he had to say the most. His words comforted her in the way that her music did. They were soothing to her soul.

27

Music is love in search of a word.

—Sydney Lanier

Jumping in her car again, Meredith drove over to the library just a few streets away and checked out a book about Mother Teresa. Once home, she put on a Chopin CD and curled up on the couch, flipping through the pages, reading certain quotes that jumped out at her from the printed page.

"You do not have to do great things. You are only asked to do small things with great love." Wow. That was powerful. There it was again. The love that had come through those magnetic eyes was written down on paper so that all could see what she had seen and felt in person. Simplicity. Living life fully could be simplistic. Everyone tried to make it complicated, but it didn't have to be that way to be done well. The rat race of life that everyone lived in was not necessary for true happiness. Scurrying around driving oneself mad with busyness was not necessarily the way to go.

She flipped through some more pages and came upon a group of quotes set aside together upon one page. They were titled "Anyway" by Mother Teresa

> People are unreasonable, illogical, and self-centered.
> Love them anyway.
> If you do good, people may accuse you of selfish
> motives.
> Do good anyway.
> If you are successful, you may win false friends
> and true enemies.

Succeed anyway.

The good you do today may be forgotten tomorrow.

Do good anyway.

Honesty and transparency make you vulnerable.

Be honest and transparent anyway.

What you spend years building may be destroyed overnight.

Build anyway.

People who really want help may attack you if you help them.

Help them anyway.

Give the world the best you have and you may get hurt.

Give the world your best anyway.

Meredith closed the book and put it down. This was a prescription for life. A prescription on how to live your life no matter what happened. It was powerful.

It was really all anyone needed, condensed so it could fit in a nutshell. Simplicity. Living life fully and with meaning could be simplistic.

28

My heart, which is so full of over-flowing, has often been solaced
and refreshed by music.

—Martin Luther

It was dark now. The wind was picking up outside probably due to
an approaching storm. The tall oaks surrounding the house stretched
out their arms as if reaching forward into the night. Their long
thin branches clothed with the now crunchy leaves of late October
scraped the windows in an eerie fashion, creating their own rhythmic
fantasy of sound. Meredith grabbed a warm wooly throw from the
couch and went out on the front porch to sit in one of the rockers
and listen to nature's symphony of sounds. The moon was full and
partially streaked with clouds, as it shone upon the empty streets and
sidewalks, where the laughing afternoon sounds of children playing
were now only a memory, as darkness and coldness replaced them
for the evening. Meredith felt comforted and at peace. The whys
and the how-comes seemed to have floated away with the howling
winds of fall that were now becoming more prevalent with the passing of the warm weather. Curled up wrapped in wooly comfort, she
rocked back and forth, enjoying the present moment of autumn in
the south.

The next day brought back the security of scheduled time and
events. Everything preplanned would proceed as expected, leaving uncertainty and the anxious feelings that came with it behind.
Breaking forth into the territory of new ideas and events could
be unsettling. Routine, although lacking growth and adventure,
brought a certain amount of comfort, despite its absence of newness
and freshness.

Meredith proceeded with her usual round of lessons. She enjoyed coaching her students, who often brought challenges to her creativity in trying to pull out the best in each individual she taught. Not everyone learned in the same manner, and she often had to explore different ways of presenting the same concepts to different people to achieve successful results.

Her agent called from New York with details and dates on her next upcoming scheduled concert. She would be playing the Rachmaninoff again with the San Francisco Symphony in late November after Thanksgiving. She had never been to San Francisco. It would be exciting to go there.

Meredith put in a call to the hospital and found out that Helen Preston had been released that morning. Following a call to their home, Bill Preston picked up and thanked her for her concern. It was acute lymphocytic leukemia as they had expected, and Helen would be receiving a round of chemotherapy shortly. After a bone marrow biopsy and a spinal tap, they felt sure the diagnosis was an accurate one. The best they could hope for was that she would go into remission. After five years of remission, the disease would be considered cured. But not everyone went into remission with the acute form of leukemia Helen displayed. Many people died of the disease. She was tired but doing as well as could be expected, and Bill Preston asked for everyone's prayers, pure and simple. Meredith said she would pass that request on to the faculty.

Remission. Her parents had never been given the gift of a possible remission.

Why were some people allowed to remain while others were snuffed out like a burning candle? Why were we not told how long our candle would burn? Why were some of us allowed to remain while others of us were taken in an instant?

What did it all mean?

29

Music takes us out of the actual, and whispers to
us dim secrets that startle our wonder as to who
we are, and for what, whence, and whereto.
—Ralph Waldo Emerson

During a break between lessons, Meredith sunk into the sensual softness of the large stuffed chair that sat in a corner space of her studio, trying to release any tension she felt. She wished the two welcoming arms of the chair could give her a comforting embrace. She looked around the room which was now still and quiet. It was usually filled with the soulful sounds of Meredith's playing or the sounds of students trying to mimic her playing. As an artist, Meredith could couple her flawless technique with expressive feeling, which came from years and years of concentrated practice. Her young students were trying to learn how to do this. The two gigantic, polished black Steinways, which were almost too large for the small studio, sat frozen in time, as if waiting for someone to bring the shiny ivory keyboards to life. Meredith loved her room, which she herself had painted a light fern green and filled with many of her personal accessories. It was her, and she felt soothed to be surrounded by the feel of its being. She needed this meaningful little corner of space that was her. She loved its quietness as much as she loved the sounds that were created here. The sounds of her music were the expression of her being. They were as much a part of her as her skin and bones were. They were her life. Much of her recent life that had meaning and purpose had happened in this very room or happened as a result of what had been created in this very room. At times like this, the silence of the room was as comforting as the sounds that often filled it. The lovely shades of greens and browns of the outdoor foliage mingled with the form and color of the large green floor plants. The hung artwork framed in black, and the nubby beige carpet brought a calmness and peace into the room that settled softly into her heart. She was at peace in the stillness.

Following the resumption of her busy schedule of classes that day, she managed to get to the little church downtown for her appointment with Father Flanagan just as he was arriving. He thanked her for her promptness and led her across the quiet street to an old brick building bearing the sign, The Georgia Cleveland Home.

Pausing on the sidewalk before going in, he shared some information about the woman they were going to visit.

"We will only stay a few minutes," Father Flanagan stated. "Margaret Clemmons is perky, smart, and full of life at eighty-six years of age, but still needs her rest. Unfortunately, she suffers from pancreatic cancer and will most likely only live a short time more. She has no family in the area, and I'm about the only one who visits her with any regularity. But you would never guess any of that when you meet her. Her life and vitality come from a strong spiritual sense of faith from within, which she has nurtured throughout her lifetime. She is as happy as a lark and looks forward to her new chapter of life after she dies. I thought meeting her might give you a new perspective on things. She lives with real purpose. She has great faith."

Upon walking inside the building, Meredith couldn't help but notice the peeling paint, the faint scent of urine, and the apparent sense of dinginess that permeated the whole atmosphere of the place. People sitting in wheelchairs were lined up along the walls of the hall like soldiers, many asleep with their heads hanging down in front of them, some drooling, and some tied into their wheelchairs so they wouldn't try to stand and hurt themselves. Smiles were absent from stoic faces attached to frail bodies overcome with problems brought on by disease and old age. *The golden years*, thought Meredith. These were supposedly the golden years in a person's lifetime. After working and living and experiencing all that the world had to offer, this was what was to crown the end of a full life? There must be a reason why all the things that supposedly mattered in life were taken away at life's end. Health and the ability and strength to pursue one's passion were out of reach for these tired, sick people. It was as if they were meant to focus their thoughts on something totally more meaningful. The entire atmosphere, however, seemed to brighten as they entered the room of Margaret Clemmons.

A tiny gray-haired woman sat in an old stuffed rocking chair in the corner of the room, writing with a bit of difficulty with fragile arthritic looking fingers in what appeared to be a journal. Her face glowed with a smile from ear to ear as Father Flanagan and Meredith entered, showing all the wrinkles which were a testimonial to a long life well lived. If she was in any pain due to her condition, she looked determined not to show it to anyone.

"Hello, Father Flanagan," she mused, focusing the beauty of her smile on Meredith as she spoke. "And who is this fresh flower I have the pleasure of meeting today?"

"This is Meredith Mason," said Father Flanagan, "a new friend of mine." Meredith smiled.

"It's a pleasure to meet you."

"The pleasure is mine," said Margaret Clemmons. "I will note in my journal that today is the day I met you," said Margaret. "I have been chosen to be blessed with a new friend, and that is a delightful gift." A love of life seemed to radiate from this woman, just as a love and knowledge of God had passed through the eyes of Mother Teresa. She was thin like a skeleton, a picture of skin and bones, yet her spirit blossomed with joy and love. Who she was inside seemed to be more important to her than anything she could do or have.

"God sends me new blessings every day, and I look forward to the day I can meet him face-to-face and receive his blessings in person. The time for me is near, my dear, and my spirit is lovingly awaiting the joy of the upcoming journey."

She is going on a journey, Meredith thought, *but without any kind of baggage. Even without mental baggage. What a beautiful picture of total acceptance and happiness.*

"Life is a gift, my dear! It is like a present. Open it with loving attention and care, and treasure its experiences with all your heart. Learn from it. Learn to be wise and gentle and giving. Take the love you have found with you when you leave because that is the treasure you have found here on earth." She put down the journal she had been writing in and carefully took out a chain of brightly colored ribbons that had been tied together.

"I am making this chain to drape the altar when my celebration of life service is held. I have carefully chosen the bold colors. They are me!" Meredith swallowed a deep breath of air and just stared at this amazing woman before her. A nurse came in to change her IV, so Father Flanagan excused himself, as did Meredith, who left with more questions but definitely with new insights.

Meredith went to her VW in the parking lot and drove away, thinking. According to Margaret Clemmons, life, whether considered by us to be happy or sad, was a gift. It was meant to teach us many things that may not have been inborn in us. It was a place to learn how to be wise and how to be gentle and how to give unconditionally to those in our pathway, but mostly to teach us how to love. The lessons learned would be needed on the next level of existence. And Margaret Clemmons believed strongly that there was a next level of existence, as did Mother Teresa. One could tell that just by looking at each of the two women. It was not only something they believed; it was something they knew. Something they really knew. How did they know? How did they know without doubtful questions? One could read about God, and one could attend a service praising God, but how did one know God? Was God love? How did one know this love?

When she got home, the phone rang, and it was Evan. "Greetings, my dear!"

"Hi, Evan. It's been an awfully unsettling day. I'm glad you called."

"I'm glad too," he rendered.

Meredith fidgeted as she spoke. She didn't know how she could put her day in to words. "I've just been upset about the Prestons and another lady I'll tell you about later. It's tormenting just watching what some people have to go through." Evan listened with his usual concern without making judgmental comments.

"Well, that has something to do with why I called. Tomorrow is Saturday, and I'd love to take you on a picnic to the mountains. I thought maybe you needed a day to relax and think and just loosen up after all of the goings on."

It was amazing how Evan could always read her—her moods, her feelings, the whole bit. He seemed to be able to pick up on her thinking without her even saying anything.

"I would love that, Evan. I really would."

"Wonderful," he exclaimed. She could picture him smiling on the other end of the phone. "I don't want you to have to prepare anything. There is a little place up here that will fix a gourmet picnic lunch for us in a basket, with dessert and sweet tea included. I will order us a basket, and it will be ready for pickup in the morning."

"That sounds lovely, Evan! Truly lovely!" Evan smiled on the other end of the phone.

"How about I pick you up at ten? That will give you a little time to sleep in and reenergize yourself."

"That's perfect," Meredith replied, really meaning it.

"Now, no chocolate chip cookies allowed, although you do make wonderful cookies!" He could hear her giggling in the background. "I just want you to be able to relax."

"And that I will do with pleasure," she added.

"Good! Then I'll see you around ten?"

"Ten it is," said Meredith. She hung up with a determination not to think of all the things that were on her mind at the moment. She took an early long bath and jumped in bed, looking forward to the much needed rest her body was longing for.

30

It is a funny thing, but when I am making music, all
the answers I seek for in life seem to be there, in the
music. Or rather, I should say, when I am making music,
there are no questions and no need for answers.

—Gustav Mahler

Golden sunshine crowned the morning as they rode most of the
way up the Saluda Grade in relative silence. Meredith just wanted
to soak in the comfort of Evan's presence. Somehow, just being with
him painted a calmness over her entire being that just made things
feel right. He seemed to automatically sense this and just drove quietly without feeling the need to speak. They both felt at home with
each other. The winding roads of the Blue Ridge Parkway led them
further upward into the heights of the North Carolina mountains
until they came to a lookout area with picnic tables and plenty of
shade. The view of the expansive countryside below was breathtaking
in the full brightness of the noontime sun. The air smelled fresh and
slightly earthlike, as Evan spread out a blanket and a few pillows he
had brought from home. He left the picnic basket of goodies in a
cooler in the car to keep everything fresh and perfect for their lunchtime meal. There was a slight chill in the air, announcing the coming
of fall to the area; and the bright colors of the leaves from a few weeks
past had turned to crunchy browns and beiges, mingling beautifully
with the blues and greens of the lower hills and valleys. Evan spread
out the blanket and propped himself up on a few pillows, inviting
Meredith to do the same. They rested quietly, taking in the serenity
of the view. Meredith stroked the two medals that hung on the chain
around her neck—the medal of St. Christopher and the medal from

Mother Teresa. They came with her everywhere she went. They symbolically told her that all was well.

Meredith wanted to talk. She *had* to talk but didn't know how to approach the things she needed to talk over without having Evan think that she was weird or strange in some way.

"Evan," she stammered, unsure of how to begin. "I've been perplexed lately. About life. About all kinds of things. I am so restless about all of this that I can't stand it."

Evan thought before answering, trying to phrase what he wanted to say correctly, all the while knowing that Meredith had been bothered by something ever since she came back from Europe. If she was having a problem, he really wanted to help her with it. He didn't want to put a damper on her talking by saying something the wrong way. He had waited for her to come to him, not wanting to force his opinions upon her.

"I've been thinking about life. About its purpose…about the purpose of our being here," she stammered, not sure of how to continue. "Do you ever think like that? Are you ever bothered by that?"

Evan thought before answering, trying to phrase what he wanted to say correctly. "I do think like that. I think like that a lot."

"Oh," Meredith sighed, somewhat relieved that he too was a thinker. "So I'm not crazy."

"No, you're not crazy," he said seriously. "I think that people who don't ever think like that must be missing something. I think we're supposed to think like that on occasion."

"Oh," Meredith said, pausing to frame her next thought.

"There are so many people. The people here now and the people already gone from their place on the earth. I can't begin to imagine why we are all here and what our purpose is here if we are only going to die and be gone."

Evan thought again, not wanting to sound trite or insignificant with his answer. "I think we're meant to learn all we can about living, which essentially involves loving. But I think we're supposed to enjoy ourselves while we're here as well. I think life is a gift, and that we're supposed to enjoy opening the gift, the gift of each new experience.

Meredith looked at Evan. "It's funny that you would say that. That's exactly what Margaret Clemmons said."

Then Evan added, "But I don't think we're ever really supposed to know what it all means. I think it's all meant to be some kind of mystery that maybe we'll really never understand."

"So it's faith, isn't it? It all boils down to having faith, doesn't it?"

Evan looked at Meredith with her wide brown eyes filled with a yearning to know and be comforted. And then he looked out at the expansive horizon. "I see the mountains. I see the trees. And I see all the beauty of this outdoor world knowing that something created it and me and that it was all on purpose and that it couldn't be otherwise. I guess it is faith. I guess we both have faith."

They relaxed quietly on the blanket and the pillows for what seemed to be a long time, resting in the beauty of nature's magnitude.

Then Meredith began again, "I've spent my whole life devoting all of myself to my music and my playing. I wonder if I've totally missed something. Did I spend too much time with my music, totally missing another part of life that is equally important? You live for almost thirty years, and it's a little disheartening to think that maybe you focused too much of your energy in one place."

Evan thought carefully and then spoke quietly but sincerely. "I think you are your music. I think you and your music are a beautiful gift to the world, and it would have been a shame if you hadn't found your music. That's who you are. But I don't think that should stop you from adding other ideas and experiences to your being. I think we are all in the process of becoming. We stop living if we stop becoming. Maybe you are in the process of discovering a new direction for your becoming in addition to the one you have already explored. I think it's beautiful. I think you are beautiful. And I feel honored that you would share all of this becoming with me." He put his arm around her, and Meredith rested her head on his shoulder. They sat for a long time again, gazing out at the horizon.

"Evan," Meredith said, "I think about old people too, old people like Margaret Clemmons. Some of them seem to lose everything when they get old. They lose their health, their strength, their ability to walk around, and even their ability to think. I've thought that maybe they have to lose all of this to show themselves or others what is really important. We all live in the rat race of life, and I think that sometimes love and kindness and consideration for others gets lost while we're trying to achieve everything else. And the loss of everything shows us that we really have no control over anything, even though we always thought we have."

They both sat for a moment, just thinking and feeling. Then Evan said slowly, "I never thought of it quite that way. I've never thought that people's oldness and loss of abilities has a purpose for themselves and others."

The sun was rising higher in the sky and was warming things up a bit. The air was clean and fresh, and all of nature seemed to be thriving beneath the delicate blue of the endless sky. The simplicity and peacefulness of nature in the raw was comforting.

"Would you like to have lunch now?"

"Sure." They both relaxed as Evan took the basket from the Jeep. They feasted on chicken salad with roasted almonds spread upon crispy croissants, scrumptious deviled eggs, potato salad, cucumber and tomato with onion salad, and iced chocolate brownies. And, of course, there was a lot of sweet tea with lemon. And it was a feast. They were both filled to the brim when everything was eaten. Evan cleaned up while Meredith thought more and gazed out at the mountains.

She began trying to put things into words again after everything had been cleaned up. "I think all of these thoughts just bombarded me after my trip to Europe. It was like a whole new avenue of thought exploded within me after my journey."

Evan smiled. "And that's a very good thing. A very good thing indeed. I think that's how we grow, if we allow ourselves to."

"Maybe you're right," Meredith added. "Maybe you're right."

They sat again, taking in the scenery, and then Meredith continued. "I always thought I've had it all together, that everything in my life was perfectly in line and that I had achieved it all, totally. And then I met the world-famous Mother Teresa and the totally unknown Margaret Clemmons, and I realized that I had only scratched the surface of my being and its possibilities with my involvement in the musical world. I think I've realized that fame or lack of it, or what other people think, has nothing to do with what is really important. My being includes so much more than I had imagined. I want to achieve the deep faith and connection to the eternal that these women radiate so beautifully. I don't have it. I'm nowhere near having it. I haven't even begun to have it, and I want to have it. I want to find it. I want it to be real. What good is all I have achieved if I have no connection to the eternal? To the world I have achieved it all. To myself, I know I have mountains to climb before I really become who I was meant to be."

Evan hugged her a little closer, and they both reclined for a long while on the blanket and pillows, looking out and enjoying the breathtaking view while taking little catnaps amidst nature's panorama of beauty. The slightly chilled late-afternoon autumn breeze picked up a bit, spreading an array of crunchy leaves upon their clothing. Obviously less bright than before, the sun was slowly making its journey across the sky to its eventual resting place in the west. The idyllic setting was hard to leave as they decided it was time to pack up their belongings and begin the long drive down the Saluda Grade back to Spartanburg and reality. They both rode back in basic silence, just wanting to be in the moment rather than contemplate the enormity of what had been discussed that day. Dusk was upon them as Evan gently brushed Meredith's cheek with a gentle kiss and soft good night. She sat on the porch rocker, watching him go, knowing that he was really not going at all. His soft gentle spirit remained with her as she knew that all would be well.

31

I haven't understood a bar of music in my life. But I have
felt it.

—Igor Straninsky

Helen Preston went into remission during the month of
November. Her family, especially Bill, was overjoyed at the thought
that the uncertainty, the imaginings of loss, and the dread of the
unknown, had at least temporarily come to a halt. In reality, the
unknown was a presence in all life, but most people preferred to not
view their daily happenings through that window. The Prestons took
their optimistic news and rejoiced in it. Margaret Clemmons was not
destined to have the same fate.

Early one November morning, Meredith received a telephone
call from Father Flanagan that she had passed away the previous
evening in her sleep, and that her funeral would be the following
day. Evan attended the service with Meredith at the small catholic
church, where barely a handful of people were in attendance. The
brightly colored ribbons Margaret had beautifully strung together
were looped across the front of the altar in the church, filling the
church with a vivid sense of her presence. Father Flanagan made the
service into a celebration of life, and spoke of the joy that would be
present as her kind, loving spirit was surely welcomed into the gates
of heaven. Following the service, the church bells rang for ten minutes, creating a special musical tribute to a lovely lady, whose life was
beautiful music to those who knew her. She had found a sense of the
spiritual here on earth, and had tried to share it with all those she had
come in contact with.

32

Music is the harmonious voice of creation;
an echo of the invisible.
—Giuseppe Mazzini

The chill of early winter was in the air. Crunchy brown oak leaves covered the previously visible grass and were occasionally blown around by the wind as it picked up a little burst of energy here and there. Squirrels scurried around searching for acorns, burying them in the ground for the bits of treasure they would be when found on a cold February day. The world was in its cyclical repetitious transition, as the routine happenings of fall would slowly but surely become those of winter. One season would follow the next, year after year, without hesitation, as sure as the sun would rise and set every day, on and on through time. Life would continue as those living it would experience its fullness as had those before them. The music of life would play on in its fervent glory.

In planning for Thanksgiving, Evan and Meredith decided they wanted to stuff and cook a turkey themselves, even though neither of them had ever cooked one before. Meredith invited five of her students to join them, who all had families living too far away for them to travel home for the holiday. They were both excited that they would have a little family to share the holiday with, although Evan said they had better be sure that they didn't poison anyone with their cooking. They did not tell these students that they would be sheer guinea pigs, as far as the cooking was concerned. Evan was a little worried about that but tried to emit pure confidence in his culinary abilities whenever he discussed the meal with Meredith.

Evan appeared one Saturday morning, proud as punch on Meredith's doorstep, with a large roasting pan in hand, only to find that it was too large to fit in Meredith's oven. After trying unsuccessfully to cram the large atrocity into the oven, they started laughing nonstop and couldn't control themselves, with Evan rolling on the floor holding his belly. Meredith felt like they would float to the ceiling in merriment as the characters in a scene from *Mary Poppins* had done when they were overcome with silliness from telling stupid jokes. The large roasting pan was definitely on the stupid-joke level of humor! Once the laughing was under control, it was decided, wisely enough, to purchase a foil pan at the grocery store and only buy a twelve-to-fourteen-pound turkey so that it would fit in the pan and the pan in the oven.

There were no classes the Wednesday before Thanksgiving, so Evan appeared early in the day on Meredith's doorstep, armed with the fixings to make a pumpkin pie. The fixings included a can of pumpkin pie mix, a tub of cool whip, and a frozen pie crust; but no one would be the wiser about how the pie had been made. Meredith was bravely going to attempt to make a pecan pie armed with her *Better Homes and Gardens* cookbook and her frozen pie crust. They were both pleased that their skills appeared to be on the same level of talent as far as difficulty was concerned. After all, what did a group of five college girls know about how a pie had been made and even about what it should or should not taste like. They had nothing to worry about!

After the pies were finished, Evan drove them both to the grocery store, where they prepared to search for the ingredients to make green bean casserole. They also picked up a few cans of sweet potatoes for another side with sufficient brown sugar and pecans for a nice toping. Evan was positive he could make the mashed potatoes and crossed his fingers behind his back as he said he had made them before. Meredith saw the crossed fingers but thought that all they really contained was a little butter and a little milk, and how could anyone mess that up without really trying? They picked out some Pepperidge Farm stuffing mix, a package of frozen Parker House rolls, a bottle of wine, and some vanilla ice cream to camouflage the taste of the pies if they really needed it. Voilà! Thanksgiving dinner was off to a fine start.

The next day, Evan dropped the turkey on the floor trying to get it into the pan, but they decided that if they washed it off, no one would be the wiser. And besides, Meredith kept her floor clean anyway. As everything began coming together nicely, the wonderful smells of turkey cooking in its juices filtered through the house and put them both in a festive spirit. The table was set with a white lace tablecloth and a set of white linen napkins Meredith had been given by her aunt. A set of little white candles in glass containers purchased at the Hallmark store were placed down the center of the table, ready to be lit when the guests arrived. They were both proud of the meal they had created together and happy that they could provide a warm, friendly holiday for a group of girls who had to be away from their families at Thanksgiving time. When the meal had been ravenously consumed, guests gone, and dishes washed, Meredith and Evan sat down on the couch in front of the roaring fire like an old married couple, too exhausted to do anything but sit in the warmth of each other's arms and bask in the contentment of a full belly and a happy heart.

The week after Thanksgiving found Meredith getting ready to jet off to San Francisco for her concert the following Saturday with the San Francisco Symphony. She would be leaving Tuesday afternoon to be present for the three rehearsals on Wednesday, Thursday, and Friday, and returning on Sunday following Saturday's evening concert. The Rachmaninoff was permanently engraved in her fingers and in her heart, but still, she practiced with fervor as if she had never performed the piece. She wanted it to be fresh and polished for her California audience. The melody "I Left My Heart in San Francisco" ran through her brain while packing and getting ready for the trip. Nostalgically, she looked forward to her trip to the City by the Bay.

Evan called Sunday morning saying he had something important to ask her and wanted to come over to personally discuss it with her. She said that would be fine. An hour and a half later, he appeared at the door with takeout lunch in hand and a smile on his face.

"This is Chinese, since you will be close to Chinatown," he remarked and pulled out two pairs of wooden chopsticks. "You can use these to wear in your hair, following our meal!" Meredith snickered but was secretly pleased with the Chinese food since she hadn't had any in a while. As they feasted on egg rolls at the kitchen table, Evan approached his tender subject with care.

"I know I've mentioned my parents to you. They live in the California mountains above San Francisco. I spoke with them over the holiday weekend. Actually it was I who called them, but that's not important."

"How did it go? Your conversation."

"They were pleasant. Actually I haven't spoken to them in almost a year, but I wanted to call them. I wanted to reconnect. I wanted to tell them about you."

"About me?"

"Yes, about you. Meredith, you know how important you've become to me. I just want them to know about you. And I thought if I told them about you, maybe they could attend your concert in San Francisco."

"Oh." She sat shocked for a moment. Not in a bad way but just thinking about meeting Evan's parents by herself, without him there.

"I've missed not having contact with them. I thought maybe if I told them about you and that you were playing with the symphony, maybe it would be a way of reconciling, a way of improving things if they met you. Two hours after we hung up, my mother called back and said they would be at the concert. She wants me to call back with the details."

"Goodness. It will seem strange meeting them for the first time without you being there."

"I wish I could be there. But I need to give exams and finish out the semester. Would you do this for me, Meredith? It would mean so very much to me."

"Of course I will. But I'll be missing you and wishing you were there. You never told me what came about with Suzanne. Did she ever reach your father to demand more money?"

"Actually, she tried to find my father but couldn't figure out where he and my mother had moved to. She's given up for now, but I'm sure that won't stop her if she needs money."

"Is there anything I need to do or say while I'm out there?"

"Not really. Things seem okay right now. I just hope they stay that way."

Meredith thought for a moment. Would things get weird if she met Evan's parents? How would she handle things if they did?

33

When I hear music, I fear no danger. I
am invulnerable. I see no foe.
I am related to the earliest of times and to the latest of times.
—Henry David Thoreau

Meredith watched the GSP airport terminal turn into a doll-house figure as she lifted off the ground in the large jet bound for Atlanta from Spartanburg. It soon disappeared beneath a sea of white clouds. She would fly from Atlanta through Houston and then on to SFO for the concert with the San Francisco Symphony. This time there was no great anticipation of a flight overseas, just the usual excitement present before playing a concert in a new and different place. The Bay Area offered much to see and do in the short time she would be there. They were putting her up on Nob Hill at the Fairmont, one of the historic luxury hotels in the city with a great view of the bay. Fisherman's Wharf, the Golden Gate Bridge, and the Redwood Forest were among her must-sees, as well as just experiencing the different cultural flavor of California. After changing planes in Houston, she put her seat back and decided to try and snooze for the rest of the trip. The three-hour time change would take some getting used to, so a nice nap would be welcome.

Meredith awoke to the flight attendant's announcement telling everyone to put their tray tables and seat backs in the upright position. Looking out the window, she saw water, lots of it, and an area of fog covering part of it. She knew they must be flying over San Francisco Bay. As the plane lowered for landing, it seemed like they were going to land directly in the water. All she could see was water until she felt the wheels touch down on dry land. Neat! It was exciting to be there. As she reached for her carry-on in the overhead compartment, she knew that this time, there would be no dramatic meeting with Mother Teresa, just a calm trip into the city. She reached down and felt the two metals hanging around her neck on the chain Evan had given her. They would always be there. They were her connection to something bigger, something greater.

The only thing dramatic about her trip into the city was the traffic! The pre-rush-hour traffic was grueling, and a lot of horn blowing accompanied the lane changing and jamming on of breaks as people switched lanes sporadically, trying to get to exits that were not very well signed. Fortunately, her driver seemed used to the daily chaos and calmly but slowly got her to the Fairmont.

The Fairmont was even more impressive than her expectations of it. The lobby was tremendous, with marble everywhere and huge displays of real flowers in gigantic pots sitting on antique tables. Potted palm plants graced the walls, giving a feel of elegance to an already elegant setting, which was scattered with comfortable couches and chairs arranged in settings suitable for chatting or having an afternoon cocktail. She felt as if she was back in the grandeur of Europe as she approached the elevator. After being taken to her room by the bellboy, she stepped out on her small balcony, which offered an expansive view of the bay. Despite there being a fog over the bay, she could see Alcatraz and the triangular shaped Transamerica Pyramid, one of the famous landmarks of the city. Behind it, the Bay Bridge could be seen in the distance, spanning the bay and leading to the city of Oakland. What she had already seen of San Francisco was very charming, and she was pleased to be here. A call to Evan revealed that his parents wanted to come in Friday evening and take her to dinner after her rehearsal.

"Oh my! Well, maybe that will be a good thing, meeting them that way."

"They seem to be looking forward to meeting you," Evan added. "I think you'll all get along fine once the initial meeting is over. My father can seem a little distant at times, but Mother loves to talk and be social."

"I hope so. It could be a long, awkward evening if we don't get along."

"Thanks, Meredith," added Evan. "This really means a lot to me. You mean a lot to me."

Meredith paused and then started rattling on about what she had seen so far. "I think I will just have dinner here at the hotel. They have a dining room on the top floor that is supposed to have great views and great food. That will allow me to retire early since my body thinks it's three hours later than it really is here."

They said their goodbyes, and Meredith freshened up for dinner. Dinner in the top-floor restaurant did reveal a magnificent view of the bay. The lights of the city sparkled in the darkness, and the Bay Bridge was outlined in white lights, revealing in the night even more the large amount of bay that it covered. Connecting San Francisco to Oakland, it was much longer than its more famous counterpart, The Golden Gate, which was on the other end of the bay, closer to the Pacific.

Meredith ordered a glass of California Pinot Grigio, along with fresh Monterey cod with vegetables and crème brûlée for dessert. Tired and stuffed, she headed for bed, thrilled to be in the city by the Bay. The weather was a little warmer than it was now in South Carolina, making it very pleasant to be here.

The next morning, she crossed the famous Golden Gate in a tour bus, heading toward Muir Woods, home of the Redwood Forest. It was so foggy early in the morning that the bridge was not visible until the bus began to cross it. The concierge said the fog usually burned off by lunchtime, and if she was lucky, she would have a better view of it by then.

Muir Woods, named after naturalist John Muir and made a national monument by President Theodore Roosevelt, was an expansive growth of old coastal redwoods, covering 554 acres of land twelve miles north of the city. One hundred and fifty million years ago, ancestors of the redwoods and giant sequoias grew throughout the United States. Today, the redwoods only grew in a narrow coastal belt from Monterey to Southern Oregon to the north due to the effects of the logging industry. They once had covered much of California. When the Golden Gate was completed in 1937, tourist visitation to the park increased tremendously. The oldest tree in the park today was 1,200 years old, but the average age of most of the trees there was 500 to 800 years old. The tallest of the trees stretches 258 feet toward the sky.

Meredith wandered through the paths in the park, stopping often to stare upward, marveling at the height of these thriving giants. The air smelled good and earthy, and the land under her feet was soft and slightly moist from the morning mist. It was awesome to think that the forest of trees was here long before the earliest days of our country when Washington was president and Indians roamed the area. The trees had lived their long lives while many generations of people had passed on. One thousand two hundred years ago was a long time. The trees had grown here in silence as the history of the world went on in other places. Wars were fought; civilizations came to power in Europe and were taken over by other civilizations. The trees grew here in silence, as day followed day and night followed night. People were born, lived their lives, and died, as the trees grew here in peace and quiet. It was kind of amazing. Life, in its totality was a miraculous event, a very complex miraculous event.

Meredith's bus dropped them off for lunch in Sausalito, a little haven for artists and craftsmen by the bay. The quaint little town with all kinds of art shops, cafes, and little nooks and crannies was nestled close to the water, with a magnificent view of the San Francisco skyline. By the noon hour, the fog had burned off and the sun was shining, revealing the bright-orange pillars of the nearby Golden Gate. Tired but happy from her morning trek in the woods, Meredith went back to the hotel after lunch for a much needed nap, looking forward to her late-afternoon practice and rehearsal with the symphony.

The late-afternoon rehearsal went well. Meredith got her usual round of compliments and praise but brushed it all off her shoulders as she took in the extraordinary beauty and size of Daniel Hall. Many levels of box-seat viewing surrounded the stage in addition to orchestra-level seating and even seating behind the lower orchestra pit. Huge sound panels hung from the ceiling, helping to create the clarity of sound heard throughout the arena from the many seats available for large audiences.

The master of a concert hall had been built in 1980 and served its location well. It was part of the San Francisco War Memorial and Performing Arts Center, being the largest of all its venues. It served the Bay Area well and contributed to the large presence of the arts in the area. Meredith was thrilled to be performing here.

34

Music must be emotional first and intellectual second.

—Maurice Ravel

As she opened the door to her room in the Fairmont, the phone rang.

"Hello. This is Jean Sanders. Is this Meredith?"

"Yes, speaking," Meredith replied with a slightly nervous feeling in her stomach.

"I'm Evan's mother. I'm here at the St. Francis Hotel. I'm so pleased to be speaking to you. I've seen your picture in the entertainment section of the paper in an advertisement for the concert."

"Yes, I guess they've plastered it everywhere," Meredith fumbled, embarrassed at the evident publicity.

"Evan has told us so much about you, and we are so pleased to be able to meet you!"

"Yes," Meredith said nervously, thinking that the meeting might be more awkward than she had imagined.

"We were wondering if we could meet you tomorrow here for lunch at the hotel. That way we wouldn't be getting in the way of your Saturday concert preparations."

"That would be nice. I'd like that."

"What if you come to the St. Francis Hotel lobby at noon, and we'll meet you there?"

"That would be lovely," Meredith said. She hung up, already feeling the stress of tomorrow's meeting.

Picking up the phone, she dialed Evan at work and was relieved when he picked up on the first ring.

"Hi, Evan. I'm so glad you're there. I just spoke with your mother, and already I'm feeling jittery about the meeting. We will be going to lunch at their hotel tomorrow. Wish we could just fly you out here for that!"

"You'll be fine," Evan said, trying to sound comforting and not revealing the little bit of uneasiness he felt as well. "They are really nice people. I'm sure you'll find lots to talk about."

"I hope so. I think after we get started, I'll be fine. It's just the whole idea of the thing. The anticipation is killing me!"

Evan smartly changed the subject. "How did rehearsal go?"

"Really well. The hall is amazing, and it will be fun doing the concert there. I feel like I could play the Rachmaninoff in my sleep by now. The challenge will be to keep it fresh, as if this were the first time I was performing it." They give me two hours of practice time in the hall before the orchestra arrives. That's really nice. I'm working under one of the assistant conductors, but he really knows his stuff and is giving me new insights.

"I'm sure you will handle everything with ease."

"Yes, if only I can handle your parents with ease as well."

"You will, and I love you for it. Gotta go…I have an exam to give. I'll be with you there in spirit."

"I know. Bye. Love you too." As she hung up, Meredith rubbed the metals of the Virgin and St. Christopher that were hanging on the chain around her neck. She knew she would depend on the two medals for her sense of confidence.

Meredith spent the next morning at the hotel and had chosen her outfit with care for the meeting and lunch with Evan's parents. Simplicity with elegance—that was her plan in choosing the navy-blue pantsuit, silk fuchsia pink blouse, and block-style navy low heels with square toes. She would accessorize with a paisley scarf of navy blues and bright pinks and wear her usual simple dot earrings. Hair behind the ears? Yes, that would be just right. Now, what if the Sanders were not simple-type people? She decided she would just be herself and not worry about them.

With that attitude in mind, she entered the lobby of the St. Francis Hotel, trying to emit the confidence she always exhibited when entering the stage for a concert. A medium sized woman wearing a silk sheath and heels was followed by a tall white-haired man. He was well dressed and approached her letting his wife go first. Well, at least Meredith had dressed properly for the meeting.

"Meredith? You must be Meredith," she said as she held out her hand with a welcoming smile on her face. Meredith shook her hand and the hand of Mr. Sanders as well, who seemed to be looking her over as if forming his opinion of her.

"Yes! And you must be Mr. and Mrs. Sanders."

"Jean and Bud," she insisted with a friendly smile.

Jean appeared warm, friendly, and motherly, as Meredith had hoped. Bud seemed to be following his wife's lead and was probably not the one who had arranged their meeting and concert attendance. Meredith inferred that he was not as interested in meeting who his son was dating. Jean seemed to be the leader, and he the slightly reluctant follower, but nevertheless he smiled kindly. Jean seemed to be the kind of person Meredith would have wanted her own mother to be, if she were still alive. Something warm and loving passed between the two women in an unspoken way, but they both seemed to be immediately aware of it and pleased that it was happening.

"Our table is ready in the dining room," Jean said politely. Let's go in and sit down, and then we can get better acquainted. Meredith followed the couple as they walked through the lobby of massive marble pillars and polished oak walls. The St. Francis was apparently another one of San Francisco's old and famous hotels.

As they sat down, Jean took the lead in starting the conversation and helped Meredith to relax.

"Our Evan tells us of your stunning career and marvelous musicianship at the piano. We feel honored to be able to come and hear you play tomorrow evening! He's told us of your recent concert in Prague. How exciting that must have been!"

"Yes, it was a great opportunity, and I was fortunate to have been invited to play there."

"And you teach as well, at a college, is that correct?"

"Yes, at Converse College in South Carolina. I'm on the piano faculty there. Working with the students gives me great purpose, but my real love is performing. I have been playing and performing practically my whole life. I am happiest when I can play and get lost in the joy of the music."

"Mr. Sanders, Bud. I understand you are a retired engineer, is that correct?"

"Yes. But that part of my life is finished now. It's good to be retired." He stopped there, not explaining what he did now. Meredith didn't ask.

Jean began again, filling in the break in conversation, "We live in the Sonoma Valley above San Francisco." It's very beautiful there. Maybe someday you can come and visit the area."

"Yes, that would be lovely."

Bud seemed slightly uneasy and anxious to be done with the lunch and the meeting. Jean kept trying to find more ways to be motherly and friendly.

"We haven't seen Evan in quite a while since we live so far away. He is our only son. I miss not seeing him more regularly. California is lovely, but we have no family here. We just have the friends we met after we came. It would be nice to have Evan come and join us out here."

Meredith felt obligated to defend Evan's life back east. "Evan is very talented at what he does at UNC. In addition to teaching calculus, he plays first cello with the symphonies in Spartanburg and Asheville."

"That's very nice," Jean replied. "He was always very musical."

Meredith smiled, not knowing what else to do or say between mouthfuls of a very delicious chicken salad plate.

"And we are so looking forward to hearing you play," Jean added. "We don't come to the city very often, but your concert has made us very happy to be here. In a way, talking to you makes me feel like Evan is here. You are very much like him."

"Thank you," Meredith answered in surprise. "I'll take that as a compliment."

After all three devoured a very nice piece of chocolate mousse pie, they said their goodbyes, and Meredith felt relieved that the meeting was finally over. The day was warm and sunny, and the fog had lifted over the bay, revealing the Golden Gate in all of its glory. She decided to walk back to her hotel and enjoy the sights of Union Square on the way.

She no sooner had gotten back to her room, than the phone began ringing. It was Jean on the phone. Bud had gone out for a stroll, and she wanted to talk woman to woman with Meredith. Meredith's stomach did a double flip-flop as she prepared to listen.

"It was lovely meeting you," she started out. I never had a daughter. I never had a pretty little girl to dress up and care for." Not sure of what she wanted to say, she went on, "I have felt badly not having kept in contact better with Evan. He is all we have. We haven't been the parents we should have been as he got older and went to college. Having a child leave home is difficult, and we failed to grasp the opportunities to keep our relationship intact. But all we can do is move forward."

Meredith just listened quietly, feeling empathy for Jean and wishing she could find the right words to help her feel better. "You seem like the perfect person for our Evan," she went on. He seemed so happy when he was talking about you on the phone. That's what a parent wants for their child—to find the right person to share his life with. I can only hope that maybe we can become closer to our Evan through all of this."

"I hope so too," said Meredith. Not knowing how much to reveal about her own circumstances, she went on. "I left home too but lost my parents near the end of college. I have had no family. So I can understand how your distance from Evan has been difficult for you."

"Oh my dear, I am so sorry! I had no idea. We will somehow have to mend this family situation for both of you. And, Meredith, tell Evan that I know about Suzanne. Bud knows that I know and I have forgiven him. Evan will know what I'm talking about. Tell him everything is okay."

Meredith heard Bud coming back in the room.

"I must go now," said Jean hastily. We will look forward to seeing you tomorrow evening."

"Thank you. I'm looking forward to it too," said Meredith.

It felt like a lead rock dropped in Meredith's stomach when Jean announced that she knew about Suzanne. Good grief. The whole thing about Suzanne seemed weird from the beginning, and now it seemed even more weird. Meredith decided not to call Evan right now. She was amazed about the whole Suzanne situation. But she guessed that they no longer had to pay her any money. Meredith decided the whole thing was something she really didn't understand, but was glad that it was over for all of them. Or was it? Mistresses and blackmail? Those were not things she was familiar dealing with. She lay down for a short nap and went to sleep wondering if it really was over or not.

35

I pay no attention whatever to anybody's praise or blame.
I simply follow my own feelings.

—Wolfgang Amadeus Mozart

Saturday evening came quickly, and with the early evening came a knock at the door and a dozen red roses from Evan. Meredith's heart skipped a beat as she placed the beautiful bouquet on a table near the patio overlooking the bay. She would call Evan later that evening following the concert. She was anxious to get to the hall for her two-hour warm-up.

Her gown was new and complimented her slender figure beautifully. Made of a dark-rose silky crepe, the gown was adorned with thin straps and a fitted bodice accented by a sprinkling of a few dark-rose sequins leading to a slightly flared floor-length skirt. Her hair would be worn up as usual. The medals would be pinned inside her dress to accompany her.

As Meredith was ready to leave the room, the phone rang. She answered it quickly, not wanting to cut her prepractice time short.

"This is Suzanne. I will be at the concert." Meredith's heart skipped a beat. She said nothing. Suzanne continued, "I know you make a lot of money playing these concerts. Perhaps you might want to share some of it with me so that Jean doesn't find out about Bud's infidelities." The phone was hung up on the other end.

Meredith suddenly felt sick to her stomach. She was good at covering up her true feelings in preparation for a performance, but this time it would be very hard to do. She convinced herself this was not her problem. Jean already knew about Bud's infidelity. Suzanne was a step behind in the game. Meredith left the room and knew that this preconcert preparation would be extremely important. But she could do it. She could leave her bad feelings behind and fully immerse herself in her music, despite the threat she had just received. She had done it before, and she could do it again. That's why she was the professional she had become. It would be okay. And it was.

Silence, wonder, stares, and then applause resounded as Meredith confidently entered the fully sold-out hall followed by her conductor. The Rachmaninoff always captured hearts and souls from the beginning, with Meredith beginning with a depth of feeling and control that always mesmerized her audience. She would live up to her billing as one of America's bright new talents in the musical world. Her good looks and classy style were secondary to the intensity of the musical journey she took her audiences on time after time. The standing ovation and thunderous applause followed by cheers of "Bravo" and "More" were evidence that she had once again exceeded all expectations of what was to be heard that evening. She avoided getting high on the compliments. She always did. It was her music that was important to her, and her thrill and joy in life was having the gift of the ability and the know-how to perform it.

Following the concert, she met Evan's parents in the lobby. This time it was Bud who approached Meredith first with a joyful hug as Jean just stood by peacefully with tears streaming down her face. It was a touching moment that could never be explained in words. He truly seemed to be delighted with her, as was Jean. Perhaps she had successfully completed her mission for Evan. They parted shortly after, knowing in their hearts that this would not be the last time they would see each other. There was no appearance by Suzanne. Was she even there?

Meredith called Evan from her hotel room following the concert. She told Evan everything. She told him about Suzanne's call, and about the good positive feelings with his parents. Evan told her not to worry about a thing. He would take care of Suzanne. And he did.

36

The music is not in the notes but in the silence between them.
                                    —Wolfgang Amadeus Mozart

The very day after Meredith got back from San Francisco, she noticed that soft, bushy large wreaths crowned with carefully made bright red velvet bows were popping up all over Spartanburg in various asunder places. Free as a bird with school closing soon for the holiday, Meredith got in the spirit of the season and went to the garden store to purchase one. The balsam fir trees were already lined up like soldiers waiting to be inspected and selected by the most particular of customers. Meredith excitedly looked forward to coming back with Evan so he could help her pick out a tree and get it home and into the house. She purchased a tree stand in preparation for the big event and even picked out a few red poinsettias dressed in crisp gold foil and fluffy red bows. The Christmas music playing at the garden store was thoroughly contagious and convinced her she really did need a few boxes of ornaments as well. When she completed all of her purchases, it took two store clerks to help her get them to the car. She laughed as she knew Evan would when she would tell him how the Christmas music put her and her money into the holiday spirit.

Meredith arranged several live balsam fir branches on the fireplace mantle and filled in the empty places with large pine cones and fat tall white candles covered with clear glass globes. The scent of the balsam filled the small little bungalow and made Meredith dig out her CD of Bing Crosby singing "White Christmas." What a thought. A white Christmas would be incredible. It almost never happened in Spartanburg, but that didn't mean it couldn't happen. Snow often seemed like a miracle. And miracles did happen on occasion!

While Meredith was thoroughly enjoying immersing herself in the Christmas spirit, a miracle was in the making. Evan was in the office of the dean of arts and sciences on the Converse campus, waiting to begin a presentation. There would be an opening in the Math Department at the college in January, and Evan was determined to secure it for himself, or at least do all that he could to try. He had been unsuccessfully checking for openings in the area the last two months without telling Meredith. This one just popped up suddenly out of nowhere, and he was delighted when he was able to land himself an interview and presentation for the position. With an advanced degree and teaching experience under his belt, he felt he at least had a chance against other candidates who would apply, and the fact that the job came up midyear might be to his advantage as well.

He was led into the dean's office to meet a gray-haired man in a double-breasted suit who seemed organized and businesslike and determined to get down to the process of the presentation rather than chat for a while about insignificant matters. The room and desk were orderly, seeming to belong to a man who knew what he was doing and worked hard at doing it. "Mr. Sanders," he stated, presenting a firm, welcoming handshake. "It's very nice to meet you and have you interested in our position." A small number of faculty still in town before leaving for the semester break were present.

Opening the folder with Evan's resume and teaching records, Dean Baker sat down and invited Evan to do the same, wasting little time in getting to the important questions and issues of the interview. When asked why he wanted to leave UNC Asheville midyear, Evan fidgeted uncomfortably in his chair and said he wished to be closer to friends and acquaintances and not to have to deal with the Asheville winter weather. Fortunately, the dean did not poke further into this uncomfortable and personal area. After further questioning, Evan was asked to begin his presentation on what he felt he could bring to the Converse Math Department. He presented the syllabus he had taught from at UNC and gave his philosophy on teaching the college student. When finished, he felt that things had gone extremely well.

The job opening was specifically in calculus, Evan's specialty, and he felt that he was a perfect fit for the job, hoping that the dean and faculty did as well. He would be taking a slight cut in salary if he landed the position, but being able to be in Spartanburg and live near Meredith was worth whatever he would have to do. He figured he could find a smaller apartment and try to cut back on expenses wherever he could. He knew he would save a lot of money on gas, not having to travel back and forth to Spartanburg from Asheville on an almost daily basis. He'd eat a lot of hot dogs and ramen noodles if he had to, whatever it took. He purposely had not told Meredith about the interview and presentation, in case the position did not come through. But he had a strong recommendation from Dr. Preston and excellent recommendations from the University in Asheville and hoped all of that plus the successful interview and years of teaching experience would secure the position. The Math Department at UNC Asheville was not pleased that he might be leaving so quickly, but his department chair understood why and highly recommended him for the position despite his disappointment. He was asked to come back in two hours while the faculty met and discussed him and his presentation.

Waiting until four o'clock would seem like an eternity. Then at four o'clock, with his nerves a bit on edge, Evan was buzzed into the office of the dean.

"Mr. Sanders," said the dean, extending his hand to Evan as he entered. "I'd like you to meet Tim Crocker, our chair of the Math Department here at Converse." Evan extended his hand to Dr. Crocker in a friendly manner. "Hello sir, it's a pleasure to meet you." Tim Crocker extended his hand as well. He seemed to be a nice guy, maybe in his early forties, who seemed pleasant and welcoming. "I understand you are interested in our math opening," stated Tim.

"Yes, very much," replied Evan.

"Usually for a position like this, we would require a more thorough presentation by you to our full faculty," said the dean. "However, this position was vacated rather unexpectedly and needs to be filled quickly before the semester is over. Your first semester will be probationary, and a full contract will be issued for the following year based on your performance during the spring semester. We feel confident with your fine recommendations, your teaching record, and your connection with Converse already that you would be the perfect candidate to fill our vacancy. Of course, your performance will reveal if that is the case. Your resume is impeccable, and we wanted to find someone of your caliber. So we would like to offer you the position for the spring semester and hope that you will accept our offer. I can honestly say I couldn't be more pleased! I was worried we would not find someone with your qualifications midyear."

"That's great," replied Evan. "I'm the one who is honored." Evan's heart was racing inside his chest, but he tried to appear relaxed and calm, shaking hands with both men in a congratulatory manner. After saying goodbye to the dean, Tim took him on a tour of the building. He would have a small office of his own, which would be nice for his books and personal items. He would teach three different levels of calculus. The beginning level was never that enjoyable because it often meant teaching students who were required to take the course but had no real interest in the subject. The two advanced levels would be great to teach. Those students would be exciting to work with since they would really want to learn all that Evan could offer them. He left the college feeling pleased with himself and buoyantly headed for Meredith's house with the good news that she was totally not expecting to hear.

He rang the doorbell to throw her off guard.

"Just a minute," he heard shouted from the back of the house. In a few moments, Meredith opened the door with a towel wrapped around her head, obviously in the middle of washing her hair.

"Evan! Hi! I didn't expect you! I'm sorry to be dripping all over the place! What brings you here today?"

"Actually I have what I hope will be some terrific news! Come sit down on the couch."

"You're keeping me in suspense. What's going on, Evan?"

"Actually, I have a new job!" She looked perplexed and a bit thrown off guard.

"What are you going to do, flip hamburgers at McDonald's or something?" she joked, feebly covering up her slightly worried wonder about what he was going to tell her.

"Okay. Are you ready for this?"

"I hope I'm ready. Tell me," she begged.

"Come January, I will be teaching here at Converse College full-time!"

"Here at Converse. Full-time? You're kidding! That's fantastic!" She threw her arms around him and gave him a teddy bear hug, wet hair and all. "How did that happen?"

"Well, I've been looking for openings for some time now, and one suddenly popped up in the Converse Math Department that was a perfect fit with my qualifications. It will be teaching calculus, which is what I love to do. I will be an assistant professor and even have my own office."

"Oh my goodness," Meredith wailed. "That means you'll be here, and I'll be able to see you whenever I can! That's incredible! So that means you'll move here from Asheville?"

"That's correct, unless I want to drive that drive every day down the mountain!"

"We are so lucky, so incredibly lucky," Meredith said. The towel fell off her dripping wet hair as she threw her arms around him, getting him thoroughly soaked as she buoyantly hugged him with glee.

Evan began combing his fingers slowly through her long silky wet hair, looking into her giant brown eyes with longing. He slowly touched his mouth to hers and gently began biting her upper lip, caressing it lovingly with each little nibble as he smoothed her hair out down her back. She was warm and enticing, and the kisses and hugs came naturally and with feeling. She was warm and cozy in a terry cloth bathrobe with smooth wet hair. Then he stopped and looked into her eyes as he cupped her angelic face in his hands. "How am I going to keep myself away from you," he whispered. "I can hardly do that even now. I love you, Meredith Mason. I love you with all my heart."

Meredith nuzzled her head into his chest and cuddled closely. "We have to do things in proper time, Evan Sanders, and in proper order. It will all happen when it's meant to," she confided as she looked up at him with honest eyes and an honest heart. They sat for what seemed a long while, cuddling closely, with Evan stroking Meredith's hair lovingly and respectfully. She was all whom he lived for at this moment, all that mattered to him at this point in time. He would do anything and be anything for her. He would wait a lifetime for her. She was his delight and his joy.

37

Music is the art which is most nigh to tears and memory.
—Oscar Wilde

The previous solitude of living alone, being alone, and thinking alone left Evan and Meredith as they went on finding each other on a daily basis in the adventure called life.

"Are you sure you need to see every tree in Spartanburg before you select one?" chided Evan. They had been to three Christmas tree yards, and Meredith was still having trouble selecting one.

"Finding a tree is a very special duty," she said, defending herself but smiling while she did it, not wanting to be difficult, just wanting to satisfy her perfectionist attitude. "Some of them have holes in them if you look at them from a certain direction, and some of them are just plain crooked. I have always liked a fat tree, but then we have to make sure it's not going to be too large to fit in the corner where we want to put it so people don't bump into it."

Evan smiled at her with great adoration and affection, thinking how cute she was being determined to pick out the perfect Christmas tree. Then he thought back through the past few years, where he hadn't even had a Christmas tree, where Christmas had been a hole between semesters that was hard to fill with anything. He thought of his apartment in Asheville and the starkness and lack of personality it had, where evening loneliness was an everyday occurrence he had learned to live with. Meredith had brought all of the joy and pleasure of living into his life, and he couldn't imagine how he had gotten along without her. Her presence made him whole and brought such meaning and contentment to his life that he couldn't imagine life without her. She was currently absorbed in thinking about the tree while his line of thinking was taking him deep into the center of his feelings. When they got in the Jeep, he put both of his hands on her shoulders and made her look at him squarely in the face.

"Do you realize what you've done for me?" She wasn't quite sure of where he was coming from, but she left all thoughts of the holiday and the tree and tried to zero in on his thinking and where he was at this time in his thought process. He became teary eyed as he went on, thinking on a deeper plane from within. Taking her hands and holding them, he continued.

"Do you realize how bland my life was before I met you, how much meaning it lacked, and how much fun and excitement you have filled it with? I just can't imagine how I went on from day to day without the prospect of being greeted by you and your cheery face each day. I know you have no idea. You have no way of knowing how it was for me, but you have just made me so happy, Dr. Mason." He squeezed the hands he held, holding them tightly.

She looked at the tears welling up in his eyes and became teary eyed herself as they shared the moment. In the past, her life had been very impersonal without him as well. She had been the envy of every young pianist, the role model for every college professor of piano. He was looked up to in the field of calculus as a professor as well. Success had found both of them in their careers, but what was that worth if life was only lived alone with no one to share it with? They both sat there in the Jeep, holding hands, with tears streaming down their faces, as other shoppers looked at them a little strangely. She got out a tissue and wiped the tears coming down his cheek. He hugged her there in the Jeep, afraid to let go for fear of losing her, losing the moment, the feeling, the whole experience. He could never lose her. She was everything that mattered to him. He could never go on like before now that he had known her. She was becoming life itself to him.

"Evan, do you remember that day in the Asheville restaurant when I told you there was a deep hurt that I had trouble sharing with you?"

"Yes, I remember very well. I never asked you about it because I figured you would tell me when the time was right."

"Well, the time is right. I want you to know. I need to share this." The tears began to flow faster, and her bottom lip began to quiver just a bit as she began.

"For a long time, I had carried a deep hurt around with me that I covered up with my music. My music had been the only thing that would temporarily take the hurt away, so I threw myself into my music, trying to free myself from the burden of this hurt. But now, with you in my life, I have come to realize how happy you have made me and how much I need you. You have filled up the aching hole with your love."

Then the floodgates broke. Years of pent-up hurt poured from her eyes and down her cheeks in the form of salty tears.

"You don't have to tell me if you don't want to."

"No, I do. I want to." And then it just came out. "I have felt responsible for the death of my parents." There. She had said it. She had uttered the words she hadn't been able to say for years. More tears followed and then a long silence.

"My parents were making the trip to Eastman for my final senior recital during a fierce nor'easter. They never made it." She stopped for a moment, searching for the right words. "They died on the highway while I was performing. Evan, for years I have felt it was my fault. They wouldn't have died if they weren't coming." It was out. Her terrible guilt was out.

"No. Oh Meredith, my Meredith. Let me hold you. It's okay. I'm here for you." She sunk into his arms and let all the hurt and anguish flow out, crying uncontrollably now.

They sat there in the Jeep for a long time, just holding each other. Finally, Evan broke the silence. "Let's go home. We have each other. We have all that we need."

38

Rhythm and harmony find their way into
the inward places of the soul.

—Plato

The Christmas spirit was definitely in the air at Converse. Classes
would end soon early in December, and there were lots of festivities
for the remaining days. The Festival of Lessons and Carols was an
annual concert of choral music and Bible readings that was beautifully done each year by the students. Meredith loved being a part of
the audience instead of having to participate on stage each year and
attended the candlelit event with Evan. It was a lovely way to ring in
the beginning of the Christmas season. Their attendance together was
noticed by Bill and Mary Preston, who smiled with approval when
they saw them together. Tim Crocker of the math faculty was there
with his wife Emily, and Evan introduced them both to Meredith.
They both knew who Meredith was from her performance with the
symphony, and they were delighted to meet her. Tim was impressed
that Meredith was Evan's date.

Evan found an apartment in the home of an older widow who
had a large home on Poplar Street in Converse Heights. Advertised
as a one bedroom and one bath, it also had a room big enough to
hold a desk perfect for a small office, a very tiny kitchenette, a private entrance, and off-street parking. It was completely furnished,
which totally suited Evan, because his Asheville furniture—if you
could call it that—was a motley assortment of old junk that didn't
match, deserving to be thrown out. Mrs. Mobley, the landlady, was
delighted that Evan was a new assistant professor at Converse and
was glad to have a male living in her quarters for protection. She

adjusted her price slightly when she found out Evan would be living on an assistant professor's salary, but she told Evan very emphatically that the rules were no parties and no girls. This tickled Meredith to no end when Evan relayed the rules to her later, making her laugh hysterically at the thought of Evan being a party boy, and at the old-fashioned sweetness Mrs. Mobley exhibited with her rules. Evan and Meredith were used to visiting at Meredith's anyway, so the antiquated rules bothered no one and kept Mrs. Mobley happy as a clam.

39

Music is the language of the spirit. It opens the secrets of life,
bringing peace and abolishing strife.

—Khalil Gibran

Evan sat in his new office in the math building with his cello propped up, playing a familiar little Bach gavotte with lightness and agility. The mellow sounds of the cello coupled with Evan's talent were a fine compliment to each other. Someone walking by in the hall might wonder why music was coming from a math office, but anyone who knew Evan would totally understand the handsome combination of his two skills. He was quite talented musically, and Dr. Preston was thrilled when he found out that Evan had landed the math position. He wanted Evan to continue on as first cello in the symphony and would pay him accordingly, which delighted Evan to no end, since his current finances had been a concern to him. Bill Preston even promised securing him some private students. Things were beginning to work out well, financially and otherwise.

Classes at Converse were finished for the semester, and Meredith worked feverishly on her next musical project, a rhapsody on a theme by Paganini for piano by Rachmaninoff. Four to six hours of practice a day was not unusual for Meredith. Strong, passionate chords filtered into the hall from her room, filled with the loving emotion that she poured into them as she played. She was in her element, and she once again got lost in the beauty of what she was creating. Her music was every bit of what she was, of who she was. It was her little piece of the patchwork of life, and she filled it beautifully with the perfection of what she had developed through a lifetime of practice and performing, of working and sharing. But knowing Evan brought a new insight into her life, a new insight of what it meant to love and be loved. She brought this new insight to her music, and her music to the world. And the world adored it.

Classes finished at UNC as well, and Evan was ready to haul what little belongings he had down the Saluda Grade to his new apartment. The fact that everything he owned fit in his Jeep showed what little he did have. He called the Salvation Army to come and take away the few pieces of undesirable furniture he had used for years, and after they had come, the apartment was bare and empty. His clothes, some music, and a few books were really his only possessions that he cared to bring to Spartanburg. He felt like he was starting a new life. It felt wonderful. A few large flakes of snow were slowly drifting from the sky as Evan carried the last of his things down the staircase and packed them in the waiting Jeep. The snow thickened as he left behind a town, a life, a way of being. He was going to Meredith. He couldn't be happier.

40

Music acts like a magic key, to which the
most tightly closed heart opens.
—Maria Von Trapp

Snow—that feathery, sparkly white stuff that fell from the sky,
brought children to ecstasy, and traveling adults to a frenzy. Why was
it so magical? In the South, perhaps part of its wonder lay in its brief-
ness—its pure, perfect, and often sudden unexpected appearance,
flake by flake, instilling in everyone the idea that life could be perfect
too. The totality of life could be pure and delicate, soft and gentle,
like a new fallen blanket of whiteness, only to yield disappointment
when it melted in a flash, leaving only puddles to prove its prior
existence. Did life leave puddles when it was gone, sometimes puddles infused with mud and debris, puddles that would drain into the
earth and become part of the whole? Was each life only an instant, a
spark in the infinite line of sparks that made up the human connection of sparks that came and went like the snow. Where did they go,
and what was their purpose? What was the purpose of Meredith and
Evan's lives as they met, lived their lives, and intertwined with each
other's? Were their sparks meant to unite in some grand purpose?
Was there a grand purpose, and if so, what was it?

Meredith got the call at 8:00 p.m., as she was merrily adding
some new snowflake decorations to the tree that she and Evan had
bought, joyously singing Christmas carols out loud with the CD
player. She almost didn't hear the ring but picked up as she turned
off the CD player. It was Spartanburg Regional Medical Center on
the phone. Evan had been riding down the Saluda Grade for the last
time. He was delightfully happy, singing Christmas carols to him-

self, knowing he was coming to be with Meredith permanently. The Jeep hit an icy patch, spun around, and hit an oncoming car on the other side of the road. The EMS report had no idea of the severity of his injuries but said Evan had pathetically and deliriously repeated Meredith's name over and over as they brought him in to the hospital. They got her phone number from information. She was the only person they could connect him to.

Nothing. Nothing could explain the feelings that slammed her in the face head-on—the panic of not knowing, the fear of what might be, the sick feeling in her stomach that stayed with her as she grabbed her purse and keys and ran to the car. Her hands shook, and her body quivered as she turned on the ignition without thought. Her life and career had been moving swiftly and perfectly on the fast track, and she had found her soulmate. She had found the person she wanted to spend the rest of her life with, and she knew for certain at this very moment that she was hopelessly and completely in love with Evan. And now life had collided head-on with their future together? There must be some mistake. This couldn't be happening. It had to be a mistake. She drove faster than she should have to the emergency room, luckily avoiding any police officers on patrol in the area. Running into the ER, she tried to find out where he was and what had happened to him at the admitting desk, but the girl on duty there had just arrived and knew nothing, appearing to Meredith to be highly incompetent, with a low level of interest in performing her job. Meredith was about to lose it when one of the EMS attendants who had brought Evan in was leaving and realized that Meredith was the woman whose name Evan had been deliriously repeating over and over.

He took pity on this woman who was shaking from fright and on the verge of breaking into tears, apologizing profusely that he was not allowed to give out any information on Evan's condition but said he'd try to get through the red tape to help her get to the doctor who was treating Evan. He disappeared for a moment while the girl at the desk sat there chewing her gum, appearing to be talking to a friend on the phone, seeming to be more interested in her personal conversation than in her job. Meredith had all she could do to relieve her frustration by insanely screaming at her, but she held her composure while waiting for the EMS man to return. The double doors leading back to the patient rooms opened, and the EMS man gestured to Meredith to follow him. They walked past rooms and rooms of patients before Meredith could see what appeared to be a doctor in green scrubs approaching the two of them. The EMS man gave her a quick hug, as if he was trying to infuse some energy and courage into her system, before leaving her to face the reality of what had actually happened. With her imagination running wild, she followed the doctor into an empty examining room.

"Are you related to the man who was brought in from the Jeep accident?" he asked, looking at her with concern, seeing the fear and worry her body language was emitting.

"I'm his only next of kin," she lied, knowing they wouldn't tell her anything if she admitted she wasn't related to him.

"Mr. Sanders has been in a serious collision with another vehicle. He is currently unconscious, and we think he has a concussion from a blow to his head. He is currently having a CT scan and some tests to diagnose its severity and any other possible problems. We do not see any outward signs of possible fractures or damage to bodily organs at this time, but we will know more when the testing has been completed." After taking her name, he led her back to the waiting room with the gum-chewing receptionist and said he would notify her as soon as he knew more. She asked if she could wait in the examining room, but he said the room was needed for a gunshot wound victim being brought in by the EMS at any minute. She nodded and took her seat among a room full of people with other assorted problems of their own.

A young baby swaddled in blankets was being soothed by a frantic mother, who seemed to be as worried about her child as Meredith was about Evan. An elderly woman sitting in a wheelchair sat with someone, probably her daughter, who visibly jumped every time her mother seemed to gasp for a breath of air. The doors from the parking lot flew open with the EMS pushing a man on a gurney, probably the gunshot victim, who may or may not have gotten into his current situation due to his own actions or to the random actions of someone else. People. They were all people at various stages of their lives. All were experiencing current stages of conflict. And at the same time, there were people in the outside world getting married. Young girls were receiving their first kiss. People were experiencing the happy moments that came to all people. Life went on in all of its glory—the good, the bad, the unexplained. All of it was happening together as the wheels of time marched on like the clock in Prague.

Then in her mind, she drew up the image of the eyes, the piercing loving eyes of Mother Teresa, the eyes she had encountered so briefly in the airport in Rome. These were the eyes that seemed to be a channel for the unconditional love of God. They were the eyes that seemed to reach out to all with mercy, concern, and understanding, trying to spread the message that all would be well and that everything good or bad had a purpose. She held the picture of the eyes in her heart and felt the mercy of a loving God surround her and hold her in the warmth of his embrace. With eyes closed, she recited the only prayer she could remember, the prayer to the mother of God himself, the prayer that came from the miraculous medal given to her by Mother Teresa that she still wore on a chain around her neck. "Remember, most gracious Virgin Mary, that never was it known that anyone who fled to thy protection, implored thy help, or sought thy intersession, would be left unaided. Inspired with this confidence, I fly unto thee, oh Virgin of virgins, my mother. Oh mother of the word incarnate, despise not my petitions, but in thy mercy hear and answer me, amen."

Meredith heard her name called from the admitting desk. She rose quickly and was led to the doctor in the green scrubs. He asked Meredith to sit down in the examining room.

"Mr. Sanders appears to have no injuries other than his concussion, which is very good news. However, he still remains unconscious, which is often the body's way of dealing with an injury of this type. How long it takes him to regain consciousness is crucial to his long-term prognosis. We will keep him here in the ER, and if he regains consciousness soon, we'll go from there. If not, we may admit him. At any rate, we will be bringing him back to this room soon. You may wait here. Do you have any questions?"

Questions. Did she have any questions? Meredith could hardly think straight, nevertheless come up with any questions of reasonable intelligence. She said no, and the doctor left to treat other patients.

Still wrapped in fear of the unknown, she tried to imagine what life without Evan would be like. She couldn't. He entered her life like a soft gentle breeze, bringing fun and warmth and intense happiness into her existence. She hadn't sought him out. He just appeared like the missing piece of a puzzle that became whole and complete after he came. She needed him. She really needed him, and this need all of a sudden became intensely clear to her as she sat here, afraid of what could or might occur in the near future.

As she sat visibly shaking, Evan was wheeled back into the room. The young men who wheeled him in left without saying anything. His eyes were closed, and other than a nasty bunch of bruises above his eyebrow and a few scratches on his face, he looked like himself. Meredith reached for his hand and held it, gently stroking the light hair on his forearm. She bowed her head and prayed her prayer of intersession to the Virgin, over and over, as if pleading with all her heart to a God she barely knew and really didn't understand. She had no idea how long she sat like that.

His arm moved slightly, and they both opened their eyes at the same time, staring at each other in silence. For the moment, Evan didn't realize where he was or what was going on, but he held her hand tightly, taking comfort in the fact that she was there.

"What's going on? Where are we?"

"You just scared the life out of me!" Meredith began smiling. She rose to place a gentle kiss on his cheek.

"That's all I need. Everything else is immaterial."

It turned out that Evan had only minor injuries from his accident, and after a night in the hospital and a good headache, Meredith was allowed to take him back to his new home in Spartanburg. The Jeep was pretty mangled up, but that did not matter to either of them. Evan was alive and unharmed despite a few bruises and scratches. She tried to drive the horrid images of what could have happened out of her mind and focused on the gift they both had been given. They were good and right together, and that was all that mattered.

41

A bird does not sing because it has an answer. It sings because
it has a song.

—Anonymous

After all the fright and fear the accident had brought, Christmas
Eve day arrived with all the delight a holiday brings to those who
welcome its coming. From inside Meredith's house came the smells
of baking gingerbread intermingled with the delightful scent of balsam. "Meredith, where is the box of raisins? We have to have raisins
for the eyes and buttons," Evan stated seriously, watching Meredith
as she placed some of the cookies onto the baking pan ready to go in
the oven.

"Oh we have to, do we, Mr. Perfectionist?" she teased. "Well,
you are in luck. I just happen to have some in the cupboard."

"I was worried there for a moment," he mused. "They certainly
would have been inferior gingerbread men without the eyes and buttons, and we couldn't have that!"

"No, never," she agreed. Evan put the raisins in place on each
cookie before the pan was ready to go in the oven. The plan was to
hang some on the tree and eat the rest during times of temptation!

"Here, let's split one of these cooled-off ones," she suggested.

"I thought you'd never agree to that," Evan mused, taking a bite
of his half of the cookie. "My mouth has been watering for the last
ten minutes!"

"Mine too," she confessed. After tasting their creations, they
strung a red silk ribbon through the small holes they had cut in the
heads of each cookie and hung them in random fashion on the tree,
creating a unique and charming look. "You better be glad you don't

have a dog. If you did, that could lead to the demise of our master-piece here!" They both laughed, and Evan gave Meredith a giant hug supposedly to praise their accomplishment, but more to just satisfy his craving to hold and be near her.

Then he walked toward the front window, opened the porch door, and told her to follow him. Stepping out from under the porch roof, down the front steps, and onto the sidewalk, he stood behind her with his hands on her shoulders and gave explicit instructions.

"Now, put your head back and look straight up." She followed his instructions just as he had told her, and after some looking, she saw giant snowflakes here and there, slowly falling gracefully to the ground.

"Oh my goodness," she exclaimed in wonder. "I don't believe what I'm seeing! I don't think I've ever seen snowflakes here in Spartanburg. This is a first!"

"And I'm so happy to be a part of a new first with you," said Evan as he grabbed another satisfying hug. The flakes slowly started coming a little faster over about a five-minute period until they were pouring down good and strong, covering Meredith and Evan's hair like a blanket. The door had been open for five minutes, letting all of the cold air in the house, so they brushed all the snow off their bodies that they could on the porch and raced inside, slamming the door behind them.

"This is incredible," Meredith remarked. "Just incredible!"

"It's an omen," said Evan. "An omen of wonderful things soon to happen!"

"And on Christmas Eve." Meredith smiled. "Snow is about unheard of down here on Christmas Eve!" They pulled a love seat up to the front window, turned it around, and cuddled up in silence, witnessing the beauty of the Christmas gift they were receiving. With her knees bent and feet curled up behind her, Meredith dozed on and off in the warmth of Evan's arms as Evan took deep pleasure in holding her as she snoozed. The snow continued to fall and fill the moment with wonder. Not only did they have the snow, but they had the gift of each other.

By dinnertime, a two-inch blanket of snow carpeted the grass and roads, making it beautiful to look at but nonthreatening to travel in. The roads were barely slushy since the temperature was hovering around thirty-two degrees. They went to dinner at Steak and Ale, the only restaurant open in the area on Christmas Eve. Meredith looked elegant in her knee-length black crepe cocktail dress. She wore a single strand of pearls, but below them, on a chain and under her dress were the two medals that had held so much meaning for her in the last few months. The medal of Mary given to her by Mother Teresa and the St. Christopher medal given to her by Evan were her treasured prizes. She felt protected by them in a similar way that she felt protected by Evan from slipping on the slick sidewalks as she clung to his arm, walking from the car to the restaurant over the slippery sidewalks. It was as if the medals protected her from the falls and spills of a life that was almost ruined by a single unexpected event that had popped up in their lives. They both had a new realization of the fragility of life and how every moment needed to be enjoyed and savored.

After dinner, Meredith and Evan went to the historic little Catholic church in downtown Spartanburg for midnight mass. The bushes and shrubs in the front of the church were lightly dusted with snow, as if dressed in lace for a fine occasion. In the sanctuary, white tapers covered with glass globes sat lit in each window, adorned with greenery and bright red velvet bows. At the front of the church below the altar was a huge manger scene with an empty crib. As the bells struck midnight, Father Flanagan walked in and placed the infant in its bed of straw, signifying that Christ had been born into the world. The choir was magnificent, accompanied by the sounds of the organ resonating in the tall archways above the pews. Evan and Meredith had never been to church together. They had never even been to a mass individually in a long time. But the beauty of it all made Meredith feel welcome and at home and especially thankful for the gift of Evan in her life. She thought of Margaret Clemmons and her strong belief in what was to come following her life on this earth; and in her mind, she saw the handmade string of ribbons that would have fit so well with the bright red and green of tonight's decorations. Evan reached for Meredith's hand and held it as they listened to the grandeur of the music and the meaning in the readings. He felt at home as well and felt thankful for his own life and the gift of being able to share it with Meredith. He, like Meredith, had come from a Catholic background long ago, and he too, felt good to be here. It felt right to both of them. They were celebrating their own love in the house of a loving God. It was Christmas; it was snowing, and Meredith and Evan had found each other.

Evan drove Meredith home in her VW, the only useful car they had between them at the moment. They sat on the street parked in front of her house, with the heat on and the motor running to keep them warm. Meredith looked at Evan as he held her hands and looked lovingly in her eyes.

"That was beautiful," she said.

"You are beautiful," Evan responded. "You are so good for me," he said. She smiled and bashfully looked down.

After sitting quietly for a few moments, she went on. "Evan, I have you. I almost thought I was going to lose you. I couldn't have stood that. I shudder to even think about it. I think about life and what it all means, and I don't understand so much about it. Yet I am so thankful for the gift that it is. Why am I so restless? Why do I have to know where it's all going?"

"Maybe you are just growing. Maybe your viewpoint has enlarged so much and so quickly to the point where you are spell-bound and overwhelmed by all that is here and all that has been here, and being the perfectionist that you are, you want to figure it all out right now."

"Maybe," she said.

"Meredith, I think about this stuff too, but I don't think there's any way that we can really know. I don't think we are meant to know. I think that might ruin our striving and our trying, our trying to sort through all the evil that exists here and search for what is good and right. I think God means for us to figure it out for ourselves, and maybe knowing what comes next would ruin all of that."

"Maybe," she quietly said.

Evan went on. "And, yes, I do believe there's a God, and that he cares for us and wants us to love this great big beautiful world he has given us. He wants us to really enjoy our time here while we use our gifts we have been given to make it a better place."

"Evan," Meredith slowly said. "Thank you for putting up with me."

"Putting up with you," he said in a surprised manner. "I love you! I love you so much. I don't think I could live without you anymore!"

She slowly raised her eyes and looked directly into his. "I love you, Evan Sanders. I love you with all of my being." He kissed her.

He kissed her passionately and lovingly there in the cramped little VW for a long time, with the Christmas snow surrounding them, pure and perfect like the love they had found for each other.

"Now," he said, when he felt he could not stand kissing her like that anymore without continuing further. "I'm going to walk you to your door and say good night because Santa Claus has to come, and he won't come if you are not snuggled fast asleep in your bed. And that's an order, Dr. Mason."

"Yes, sir." She smiled. He opened her door, walked her up the steps, and kissed her cheek softly when she was safely inside. She watched him get in the VW and drive away, making tracks in the snowy road.

"I love you, Evan Sanders," she whispered softly. "I really love you." Tonight was the first time she had spoken these words out loud. And she meant them with all her heart.

Christmas Day dawned in Spartanburg with a covering of white on the ground and a bright golden sun shining on the stark but snow-covered branches of the trees, making them sparkle and dazzle like stars. Evan appeared like Santa Claus at Meredith's door that morning, loaded down with packages and beaming with a love that came from deep within him. Meredith made Evan open his first. She had gotten him a tan V-neck cashmere sweater and a smart-looking leather briefcase for his new job, along with a handsome pure silk scarf for his dress coat and a new pair of fine leather gloves. Evan smiled and then enjoyed watching Meredith open a cowl-neck sweater of lamb's wool from Talbots and a brown leather shoulder bag to replace her worn-out one, along with bath powder and cologne by Estée Lauder. An exchange of hugs and kisses followed the gift giving.

Then Evan got serious. "Meredith, there is nothing I could give you that can explain the feelings inside of me you have brought to my life. You have shared your soul with me and have changed my life forever." Evan teared up as he reached in his pocket and pulled out a small black velvet box. Meredith's eyes filled with tears as she saw the box in his hands. Evan's strong big hands were shaking as he opened the box.

"Meredith, I need you for my wife. I feel ecstatic to have found my soulmate." Evan reached for the one-carat pear-shaped diamond ring and placed it on the fourth finger of her left hand.

"Say yes, Meredith. Fill my heart with unending joy and say yes. Marry me!" Meredith looked at Evan with her luminous large brown eyes, and Evan knew her answer before she uttered a word.

"I will be yours forever, Evan Sanders. I love you!"

42

Music is an agreeable harmony for the
honor of God and the permissible
delights of the soul.
—Johann Sebastian Bach

All the questions of life and meaning may not have been answered or realized, but Meredith and Evan knew that they would have a lifetime together to figure them out. They were married two weeks later at the little Catholic church in downtown Spartanburg by Father Flanagan, with the music of the Converse String Quartet echoing through the tall archways of the old church. Evan's parents flew in from San Francisco and were present for the ceremony. Beaming with pride and with tears streaming down their faces, they sat in a front pew, with hopes for a new loving family life in the future.

Evan and Meredith honeymooned for a long weekend in the mountains of Asheville, contemplating all that was still to be discovered as they explored the years that lay ahead of them. They were soulmates, and they knew that they had found a jewel in each other that was brighter and more meaningful than the one that Meredith now wore on her finger.

CODA

A New Beginning

Classes for the new spring semester began with Evan in his new office in the math building and Meredith in her studio in the music building. There was by far more excitement in the music building, as everyone who came by Meredith's office had to fawn over the new diamond ring and wedding band she now proudly wore on the fourth finger of her left hand. The light from the rising sun through the picture window in Meredith's studio hit the center of the diamond and made sprinkles of diamond dust dance all over the ceiling. Who could make music while watching the extended light show? And who could concentrate with the level of excitement that was floating through the room?

Meredith herself felt different too. She was a married woman. Going home was now an excitement, instead of just a blah ending to her day. Having someone to come home to or having him come home to her was fulfilling. For Meredith, it was like she was coming home to her other half. It was the other part of her, the part of her that was always missing but that was genuinely necessary for her total fulfillment. The house felt warmer and happier. Even if they just sat there in silence, reading or working apart from each other in the evenings, there was a togetherness between Evan and Meredith. It was a togetherness that made her feel whole and accepted, needed and wanted. They were mates. They belonged with each other and to each other, and they knew it.

And then there was the sex. The gentle touching and melting of bodies, one into the other. It was a new way of totally giving to each other. It was a new way to speak without talking. It was a way to totally become one with the other and to blend souls. It was holy. It was a gift from God meant to unite their spirits physically and bind them together forever. Sharing had a new meaning. Giving and receiving had a new meaning. And it was beautiful. Evan was the gentlest and most considerate of husbands and always treated Meredith with great honor and respect.

She loved being with him and having him hold her in his arms. She felt safe and wanted.

Marriage was about bringing out the best in the marriage partner. Meredith felt prettier, more confident and self-accepting, and just plain special when she was with Evan. Life was just more fun with him. Knowing that she was cherished for who she was, and that she always would be, brought a sense of comfort and peace to her life that hadn't been there before. She felt he brought out the kindness in her soul and helped her to have more empathy, not only with him but with the rest of the world. They helped each other to become better people.

Evenings were the best part of the day. They both looked forward to them. Evan entered their home on Palmetto Street and was greeted with, "Welcome home, Mr. Sanders!"

"Thank you, Mrs. Sanders," he beamed, giving her a big hug and generous kiss. She was technically still Dr. Mason, as she would keep her own name for professional reasons, but he liked the ring of "Mrs. Sanders." He liked having a "Mrs. Sanders," even if it was only his pet name for her in private.

Theirs was definitely a present-day marriage. Meredith could never be home in time to have a sumptuous dinner waiting on the table for Evan as he arrived home. Nor would he have wanted that or have been able to do that for her. They did things together and shared chores together. They were equal partners, each taking responsibility for whatever had to be done. Evan could clean a toilet as well as he could grill a steak. Meredith's new surge in performing opportunities made it affordable for them to eat out when they cared to, but tonight she had picked up some hamburgers to grill on the way home. Potato salad and green beans would round out the menu.

"I'll do the hamburgers or the green beans," Evan shouted from the bedroom as he changed into a pair of cutoffs and a T-shirt. "Take your pick."

"You're the grill king." She laughed. "I'll get the beans and set the table."

Would there be children? Meredith and Evan had discussed this subject many times at length but had never come to any decision. They both loved children. Meredith could see Evan as the perfect father, but although he had a great love for little people in general, he realized he had not had a role model to show him how to be the perfect father. And that bothered him. Meredith tried to assure him that that would make him a better father, as she knew he would try doing his very best in fathering because that was just the type of person that he was. But he still had his misgivings. Meredith had not really had a perfect role model either for being a mother, but she insisted they could invent their own path as they went along. And then there was Meredith's job. Her incredible surge in performance offers would keep her away from home a good bit, at least for the present. She had hoped she could bring Evan with her on some of the trips at some point, but with his new job at Converse, that was highly unlikely, at least for the present. But maybe that would work out some time in the future. She could not see leaving a child with a nanny all of the time, so for the present, they decided that they needed time to enjoy each other and put any baby making on the back burner at least for the present.

On the first-month anniversary of their wedding, Evan knocked on the door loudly, which surprised Meredith because he always just came in since they had been married. When she opened the door, there he was, holding a chocolate lab puppy in each hand, being licked to death as he held on to each one tightly. Meredith's heart just melted as she took one from his hands before he dropped the two of them. It began licking her face gleefully, wagging its tail with full force and wiggling happily as she held him.

"Happy anniversary," Evan announced with pride, his dimple punctuating the wide smile he held on his face.

"Oh, Evan!" How precious they are! And they're so soft!"

Meredith and Evan sat down on the floor with the two little puppies climbing all over them and each other as well, playfully frolicking with the energetic joy only a new puppy could exhibit.

"We have one girl and one boy! I thought we should keep the count of the sexes equal in the Sanders home, at least for now."

They sat on the floor and played for what seemed like hours.

"Are they potty-trained?" Meredith asked? No sooner did she say that than the female puppy squatted and peed all over the floor.

"I think that answers your question." Evan laughed. "Let's put them on their leashes and take them out for a bit."

Evan pulled out a pink leash and collar for the girl and a blue leash and collar for the boy. As the puppies pulled and tugged, Meredith and Evan had all they could do to hold on to them as they all went out the door and down the stairs. It could hardly be called a walk that they went on. Maybe calling it a drag would be more appropriate, but nevertheless, the two pups did their business many times and sniffed at what all the other dogs had done as well.

Life went on in the Sanders home, with two little pups to come home to. They were all definitely a family now. Two furry, growing children added to the fun of coming home.

Life was good. They each made it good for each other.

Epilogue

Meredith's fame as a pianist only increased, bringing her concerts in London, Vienna, and many other interesting parts of the world. Evan would accompany her on the trips when time allowed, but his main focus was teaching calculus at the college. He eventually became a full professor, with the total respect of students and faculty and continued playing the cello with the symphony, enjoying giving lessons to young cellists on the side.

Within a few years, Evan's parents decided to move to Spartanburg from California and bought the house Evan and Meredith had lived in on Palmetto Street, which was an adorable but small house. Having his parents in town brought a sense of family to their lives, which made holidays and weekends more special. Jean Sanders brought a motherly warmth to the family and even managed to crack Bud's businesslike exterior, helping him to appreciate family as she did.

Evan and Meredith bought a lovely brick Georgian on Otis Boulevard, having it fully renovated and modernized before they moved in. After six years of marriage, Elizabeth Rose Sanders was born and became the delight of their lives. Meredith adapted her schedule when little Rose arrived, still teaching and concertizing, but in a modified way. Jean was thrilled to become a doting grandmother and jumped in whenever she was needed.

Evan had said he would take care of Suzanne, and he did. She was out of their lives forever. She was charged with blackmail and suffered the consequences of what she had done.

There was less time to contemplate the questions that had filled Meredith's mind before her marriage. Both Evan and Meredith became caught up in the busyness of life, the busyness of being parents while having active careers and fulfilling family lives, as generations before them had done. They all lived to support each other, to help each other grow, and to become better people. The questions would return, as old age would inevitably creep in upon them, and life would surely slow down as it had for generations before them, giving them more time to think and ponder and wonder. Would the answers be there? Probably not. But the presence of a strong faith built from years of living, praying, and experiencing, would assure them that there was more to come when their lives on this earth came to a close. Faith—faith as Evan had said on that mountaintop long ago—it all would come down to faith.

About the Author

Gail Miller Mahaffey is a retired elementary music specialist. For over thirty years, she has written and directed her own musicals and plays onstage for young children. She is currently a church organist and cantor. She lives in upstate South Carolina with her husband and her beloved golden retriever, Maggie. *Music of the Soul* is her first novel.

CPSIA information can be obtained
at www.ICGtesting.com
Printed in the USA
BVHW082148080621
609007BV00004B/397